Elaine Edwards v
various aspects of
the UK. This is her first (and probably last!) foray into
writing: when she met Stephen, he proclaimed that they
would work together in the future ... but she didn't realise
that this is what he had in mind.

Stephen Jarvis was born in Essex and is probably the
world's leading expert on unusual leisure activities: he is
the author of *The Bizarre Leisure Book* (Robson Books,
1993) and is a frequent contributor of articles about off-
beat hobbies to British national newspapers, including *The
Times* and *The Daily Telegraph*. This book is about his own
unusual leisure activity.

Also by Stephen Jarvis
and published by Robson Books

The Bizarre Leisure Book

The Kissing Companion

Secret Techniques of over 500 Exotic Kisses

Stephen Jarvis and Elaine Edwards

Robson Books

First published in Great Britain in 1997 by Robson Books Ltd,
Bolsover House, 5–6 Clipstone Street, London W1P 8LE

British Library Cataloguing in Publication Data
A catalogue record for this title is available from the British Library

ISBN 1 86105 135 2

Photoset in Palatino by Columns Design Ltd., Reading.
Printed in Great Britain by Creative Print & Design Ltd.,
Ebbw Vale, S. Wales.

DEDICATIONS

Elaine: To my Mom and Dad, Peter and Jeanne Edwards.

Stephen: To my friends, Marcus (The Marquess of Darkness)
Forest and Patrick Johnston.

PREFACE

We were kissing in a pub and someone said, 'Oi, you two, stop that!' Little did they know we were doing research...

Our interest in unusual forms of kissing had begun a few months earlier, when we switched on the TV to catch the last ten minutes of a wildlife documentary. Two hippopotamuses were threatening each other; and we started copying the creatures: snorting, dropping our jaws, and putting gaping mouths together ... and thus, the **Hippo** kiss was born.

In the next few weeks, we invented other unusual kisses: we spent a hilarious evening doing the **Passionless** kiss; then came **Hannibal Lector, Tunnel of Love, Timeless** and many more – and we started stringing together sequences of kisses, calling out their names before doing them, one after another. Then one day we were on the number 70 London bus, and we suddenly wondered: 'Would it be possible to write a *book* of different types of kisses?'

To some people we told, the idea seemed ludicrous – would there be enough material to fill a single page? ('I thought there were only two ways of kissing,' said one person – 'you either put your tongue in, or keep it out.') But over the next few months, we created, or discovered, *hundreds* of variations: we sat in front of mirrors to analyse the possible movements of lips, tongue and teeth; we spent days in libraries researching into the history of kissing – it came as a shock to discover that the Victorians, in spite of their reputation for prudery, were great kissers, and invented many variations as parlour-amusements. We also visited London Heathrow – the world's busiest airport – to observe the kissing at Departures and Arrivals (which was great for finding alternative methods of blowing a kiss). Before long, we had a repertoire of kisses of every conceivable kind: romantic kisses, sexy kisses, silly kisses, kissing-games, kisses from different cultures, stupid chat-up lines for kisses, cocktails and recipes called 'Kiss', optical-illusion and conjuring kisses, uses of the 'X' symbol to represent a kiss ... we could go on. We believe that the result of all our investigations – this book – is the most extensive analysis of kissing ever written. In a way, the book is a manual of tricks, such as you might find for skateboarding or juggling – only, kissing-tricks are easy, and very cheap to do: after all, everybody owns the equipment.

Perhaps the best method of using this book is to sit with your partner, open the pages at random, and just try out the first kiss you see; some complicated kisses are indeed 'scripted' for such occasions, and require both partners to role-play, following the instructions. At the other extreme, you will find very simple kisses that work best as part of a medley: on their own, such kisses are not especially significant, but put them together in rapid succession with others, and you can become a quick-change artist of kissing. However you use it, we hope that this book will inspire you to come up with unusual kisses of your own – there are infinite possibilities. Indeed, if you and your partner use a kiss which isn't listed in this book, then please write to us about it: we are still collecting kisses and may want to produce a follow-up book!

You could also say that our aim is to undermine the most famous of all statements about kisses: namely, the line from the song 'As Time Goes By', in the movie *Casablanca*, which is sometimes quoted as 'A kiss is still a kiss' and sometimes 'A kiss is just a kiss' – but either way, the song's suggestion that a kiss is unvarying, unchanging and eternal is something we regard as a source of shame, not pride. As we move towards the new millennium, it's high time to re-invent and re-invigorate the kiss!

Finally, thanks to the following people for contributing kisses to the book: Clare Eltis, Fouad Nouar, Karen Collier, Paul Hilly, Joan Jarvis, King Leo of Redonda, Alan Elsey and Kari Barth. Thanks also to Philip Eckstein for the loan of his computer.

Stephen Jarvis and Elaine Edwards

Absolute Kiss

Your partner is sitting down, and you straddle their legs. Kiss them with amazing passion and intensity, but the important thing is to run both your hands over their face, so as to know every detail of their features. Once you have done this kiss – which might be characterised as 'normal' but 'extreme' – you are ready for the other variations in this book.

Absolute Zero Kiss

Lick an area of the kissee's cheek or hand, then open your lips and apply them *very* lightly to the area. Breathe in deeply: cold air will rush in and chill the area, and this chill will linger for a while after your lips have been removed from the kissee's skin. This is a powerful kiss, which can be used once in a while to playfully 'shock' your partner.

Alphabet Kiss

Stand close to each other. Both of you go through the alphabet mentally, with eyes shut. When you reach the letter 'X' extend your lips and make a kissing sound. Is there a pair of lips to meet you? If not, say 'Y...Z' mentally, then go through the alphabet again – but adjust the speed. (Your partner's peck, when it comes, will help you to get the right speed – but of course, you may still over-adjust or under-adjust.) The aim is to keep on going through the alphabet until you both reach the 'X' at the same time, and your lips meet in a kiss.

Angel's Kiss

- $\frac{1}{4}$ oz white creme de cacao
- $\frac{1}{4}$ oz sloe gin
- $\frac{1}{4}$ oz brandy
- $\frac{1}{4}$ oz light cream

Pour ingredients into glass in order given, layer upon layer, to make a pousse café. (If you pour each layer over the back of a spoon, the layers will be more defined.)

Angle of Inclination

Lick just the corners of your partner's mouth. For some people, the corner is a highly erogenous zone.

Apple Phyllo Kisses

This makes 8 filled pastries:

1 cup	Cooking apples, finely chopped	250 ml
1 tsp	Lemon juice	5 ml
$\frac{1}{4}$ cup	Cheddar cheese, grated	50 ml
1 tbs	Fresh chives, minced	15 ml
4 sheets	Phyllo pastry	4 sheets
$1\frac{1}{2}$ tbs	Melted butter	20 ml

- In a small bowl, combine first four ingredients and set aside. Preheat oven to 375 deg F/190 deg C.
- Cut each square of phyllo in half lengthwise and into fourths crosswise, forming 32 6x4-inch squares.
- Lay a square of phyllo on a sheet of waxed paper. Brush lightly with melted butter. Repeat with two more squares of phyllo.
- Place two tbs of filling in centre. Bring up opposite corners of square and pinch to form a kiss. Repeat with remaining phyllo, making eight filled pastries
- Transfer to lightly buttered baking sheet. Bake for 15 to 20 minutes, or until golden brown. Serve warm.

Atishoo-A-Kiss-You

If you see your partner about to sneeze, then say a number aloud, such as 'Five!' and try to kiss them five times before the sneeze happens. Can you achieve your goal and escape without being sneezed on? (For more fun, try to achieve higher and higher numbers.) Incidentally, there is an old saying that if you sneeze on a Tuesday, you will kiss a stranger ...

Attack of the 50-Foot Woman

Approach your partner and see your face reflected in her eyes. Now close your eyes and imagine that you are as small as your reflection. Your partner then takes the tip of your little finger in her mouth and you imagine that, with one 'kiss', she swallows your whole body. (This might seem a very strange kiss-fantasy to act out; but actually, there are several specialist newsletters published in the USA for people who do indeed fantasise about partners who are as massive as fairytale giants.)

Aural Pex

Stand behind your partner. They turn their head alternately to left and right so that you can plant a series of pecks on both of their ear lobes. This should send tingles down both their legs. Alternatively, place your lips right against the opening of your partner's ear. Whisper – very softly – 'I love you', with your lips still touching the ear. Try it – this will give your partner goosebumps.

Australian XXXX

Go to the fridge, open a tinny, and apply to your, and your partner's, lips.

Bacchanalian, The

Feeling decadent? Squeeze the juice from a bunch of grapes over your partner's mouth. Then move in for the kiss, lapping up the juice.

Balinese Kiss

The Balinese bring their faces sufficiently close together to feel the warmth of the skin. (They then inhale to smell their partner's fragrance – of course, in Western societies, this can be the fragrance of perfume or after-shave.)

Baseball Pop Fly

A stylish way of blowing a kiss. The kisser kisses his/her fingertips, then 'drops' the kiss from the fingers and pre-tends to swing an imaginary baseball bat. He/she makes a click sound with the mouth to represent the ball – that is, the kiss – being struck; the kissee pretends to catch the invisible ball and brings it down to the mouth. The first time you do this you will probably have to call out to the kissee as you bat, telling them to catch the kiss and bring it down to their mouth – but afterwards, the convention should be established.

This was a forfeit used in Victorian party-games. The 'beggar' has to fall on his knees before a lady, imploring for charity. She says, 'Do you want bread?', 'Do you want water?', 'Do you want a penny?' and so on. To all these questions, the beggar responds by shaking his head impatiently. Eventually, the lady says, 'Do you want a kiss?' and the beggar jumps up and accepts the offer. Of course, one of the ways in which this (and other forgotten kisses) might reappear in the modern world would be for you and your partner to simply open this book at random and act out the first kiss you see. (And so work your way through the book.)

Bent Kiss

Direct from the pages of the *Kama Sutra*: 'When the heads of two lovers are bent towards each other, and when so bent, kissing takes place, it is called a 'bent kiss'.' But, judging from our experience, the only fun you're likely to get from this kiss is trying to figure out what is meant by 'bent' here – just how are you supposed to place your heads?

Betty Blue

Put on *way* too much lipstick: make your mouth twice the size – almost like a clown – get lipstick on your chin, go *wild* with lippy. Then kiss your partner! Both rush to a mirror for a guaranteed laugh.

Bewitched

There are some kisses which are of no particular subtlety if performed on their own, but which can be fun if performed as part of a rapid *sequence* of different kisses: you call out the name of the kiss, do it, then move swiftly onto the name, and performance, of the next kiss in the sequence – the idea is to dazzle by demonstrating the *range* of kisses at your disposal. 'Bewitched' is a perfect example of a kiss that might be used in such a sequence: one, or both, of the partners simply twitch noses while kissing!

Biceps Curl Kiss

And here's one for partners who enjoy working out together. Both do a 'biceps curl' exercise, face to face. (Stretch out your arms horizontally at your sides, bend them up at the elbow, so that your forearm and upper arm form an 'L' and a mirror-image of an 'L': this is your starting position. Then bring your forearms forward, so that they are in front of your face. Now return them to the starting position. Repeat this quickly.) To turn this into a kiss, lean forward when your forearms are back, and bring your mouths together. Kiss at the same point on each repetition of the curl.

Big Bad Wolf Kiss

This is a version of a blown kiss, in which the blowing is exaggerated out of all proportion. Peck your palm, then *really* fill those lungs with air, let your partner *hear* you sucking up all the oxygen in the room. Expand your chest and cheeks to bursting-point – and with one almighty hurricane-blast, blow that kiss from your palm to your partner until you are bent double, completely spent.

Big Slurp, The

Some people love to feel a wet tongue moving over their face, others just find it slimy and disgusting. The Big Slurp is the ultimate for tongue-lovers: *completely* wash your partner's face with your tongue and let it air-dry.

Blink, and You'll Miss It

You stand studying your partner's face. You examine every feature: eyes, forehead, lips. You breathe gently, you stroke your partner's cheek, you give every indication of being madly in love. And then you go and spoil it with a very quick peck! (Once in a while, an anti-climax can be almost as much fun as a climax.)

Blood Kiss

Note: In the age of AIDS we emphatically do not approve of any kiss which draws blood – however, blood kisses have been mentioned in romantic novels and some people are sure to try them out. If you are going to do this with your partner, make certain that you both have an HIV-test first. Nibble and bite your partner's lower lip until you draw blood – then swallow it.

Bloodhound

One person dabs a spot of perfume somewhere on their body. The other person then has to sniff out the location of the perfume-spot, moving mouth and nose along their partner's body. It might take a while – and remember, you have to reward a good dog.

Blow in my Ear and I'll Follow You Anywhere

Person A pinches the nose of Person B, and blows into B's mouth. A then pivots head to let B blow the air into A's ear. A bizarre kiss – if you do it in a public place, you'll get a few looks!

Bodice Ripper

Open a trashy romantic novel and find a passage that describes a kiss. You and your partner then attempt to re-create the smacker: hold the book while you're kissing and break off every few seconds to read the next bit of the description – 'He devoured her …' 'He sucked the life out of her …' 'Their tongues battled …' And so on.

Body-Painting

One of the most erotic of kisses. Let's say the female partner is naked: she raises her finger to the lips of her partner, thereby moistening the fingertip – and she proceeds to 'paint' her own mouth, and then the intimate parts of her body, with her partner's saliva, while he looks on.

Body-Pun

Start giving little kisses to the muscles of your partner's chest and say, 'Do you know what these are? They're pec(k)s.' Stifle your partner's groan with a kiss on the mouth.

Bogie and Bacall

This 'scripted' kiss recreates a classic movie scene – it is done when the male partner is unshaven. Kiss, rubbing cheeks together, then 'Bacall' says, 'Oh I liked that … except for the beard.' She strokes the bristles and says, 'Why don't you shave and we'll …' She slaps 'Bogie's' face and adds, 'Try it again.'

Bornean Kiss

In some languages the very word for 'kissing' means 'smelling'. For instance, Borneans do not 'greet' but 'smell' a visitor; and a Bornean parent will show affection by burying his/her face in the neck of a child and drawing in a long breath through the nostrils. So do this with your partner … and become a Bornean 'wild-man'.

10

Bouncing Bread Roll Kiss

You are seated opposite each other at a table. You say, 'There is a Jewish custom of kissing bread before eating it – but my kisses are so powerful that they can make bread bounce.' Then raise your foot off the floor and kiss a bread roll. Hold the roll in your hand as if you are going to throw it on the floor – your hand, with the roll in it, travels below the table and, at the same time, your foot hits the floor, to create the sound of the 'bounce'. Then, with your hand concealed below the table, throw the roll into the air with a flick of the wrist – do not let your partner see your forearm move. Then catch the 'bouncing' roll and pass it to your astonished partner.

Bouquet of Balloons

This is an alternative to a dozen roses ... and come Valentine's Day, it's a lot cheaper! Buy 12 balloons, kiss each one to leave a lipstick mark, and present them to your partner.

Brand X

Say to your partner, 'Brand X!' – crossing your index fingers to make an 'X', and applying the 'X' to your partner's body like a branding-iron. As you do so, go, 'Sssss....' as if searing the flesh. (Do this anywhere on your partner's body – though an obvious place is the rump.)

Breezin'

This is more jazzy than an ordinary blown kiss. Cup your hand over your ear, thumb just behind earlobe. Then, keeping the thumb in a fixed position, swivel the fingers towards your mouth and at the same time turn your head so that it is almost horizontal and parallel with the fingers. Then kiss the air and blow. This can very effective if you corkscrew your body around – you might have been facing away from your partner, but you turn back to blow the kiss.

Brief Encounter

Say in a cut-glass English accent, 'Oh! Oh! I've got something in my eye!' It's a ruse to get your partner to look in your eye … and then, of course, you can kiss them.

Broken Heart

An impressive optical illusion. The kissee holds both index fingers horizontally at eye level about six inches from his/her eyes, the fingertips about an inch apart. If he/she now focuses beyond the fingertips, a floating disembodied 'sausage', made from the fingertips, will appear in mid-air. If kissee now adjusts the fingers slightly – bringing the hands closer together, so that the fingers form an arch – it is possible to turn the sausage into a flesh-coloured floating heart. Kisser then approaches. Initially, the heart will seem to be on the kisser's nose, but as the kisser's face comes forward, the heart is 'broken', or disappears. The kisser can, of course, create a heart of their own if desired, and kiss through it.

Bus Stop

If you are both at a bus-stop, then one person waits until a bus comes into sight and says, 'Here comes the bus(s)!' That person immediately plants an ambiguous kiss. We've found that not everyone knows that the word 'buss' means kiss – who would have thought that kissing can improve the vocabulary?

Caligula Kiss

The insane Roman emperor Caligula would extend his middle finger to be kissed which then (as now) was a rude gesture. Use this, for example, when you have won a point in an argument, and are feeling imperious.

Can You Believe It Kiss

The idea of the 'Can You Believe It Kiss' is to kiss your partner, tell them a strange fact about kissing, and kiss again. Here are a few examples of facts you can use – but if you watch the newspapers, you will undoubtedly find material for new kisses of this sort.

A man in Australia was awarded $142,000 after a car crash left him with numb lips, which meant he was unable to enjoy the delights of kissing.

The University of Arizona Poison Control Center's 1990 study of 218 rattlesnake bites recorded a case of a man who was bitten on the tongue while kissing a snake.

According to medical research, kissing can lead to head lice, passed on when you touch heads.

In November 1996, a woman from Edmonton, Canada, was accused of biting off a piece of her boyfriend's tongue and flushing it down the toilet when he tried to kiss her during an argument.

Canned Heat

Give this a try: you and your partner wear portable stereos, but one person listens to heavy rock (such as Led Zeppelin's 'Whole Lotta Love') and the other listens to something extremely romantic (such as Celine Dion's 'Falling Into You'.) Kiss in time to your respective songs. For an added extra, try to guess what your partner's song is. And, as an interesting variation, you might try the 'Sound of Silence' Kiss: you both have to *imagine* different tunes, with no personal stereos allowed.

Captain Hook's Hand-Kiss

Pull your hand inside the sleeve of your sweater, but leave your index finger exposed and curled up like a hook. Ask your partner to give the finger a kiss. Another good 'sequence' kiss – see the note on the **Bewitched** kiss.

Caribbean Kiss

- $\frac{1}{3}$ oz dark rum
- $\frac{1}{6}$ oz amaretto
- $\frac{1}{6}$ oz Kahlua
- $\frac{1}{3}$ oz cream
- cinnamon/ brown sugar for decoration

Dip rim of glass in Kahlua then into brown sugar. Shake spirits and cream with ice. Strain and pour into glass. Sprinkle with cinnamon.

Carmen Miranda

Some kisses, like this one, emerge from spontaneous silliness – and for some reason, the kitchen is a place that's particularly conducive to this type of behaviour. So, simply take a piece of fruit that happens to be at hand, place it on your head and start to sing 'I-I-I-I-I like you very much,' and kiss your partner to finish. (Best performed with a banana, which will balance nicely on your head.)

Carob Kisses

Nut Pastry

1 cup	Wholewheat flour	125 g
$\frac{1}{4}$ cup	Bran	25g
1 tsp	Baking soda	5 ml
$\frac{1}{4}$ cup	Margarine	25 g
$\frac{1}{4}$ cup	Ground almonds	25 g
$\frac{1}{4}$ cup	Unsweetened chestnut puree	25 g
2 tsp	Lemon juice	10 ml
half	Lightly beaten egg	half
$\frac{1}{3}$ cup	Yoghurt (low-fat)	80 ml

- Mix together the flour, bran and soda. Rub in the margarine. Add ground almonds and chestnut puree. Mix the puree well into the flour mixture because it can tend to stick in one lump.

- Add the lemon juice, egg and the yoghurt to make a soft dough. (You may need a bit more yoghurt if it is too dry).

- Chill for 30 minutes before using.

Carob Fudge Icing

$\frac{1}{4}$ cup	Carob powder	25 g
$\frac{1}{4}$ cup	Margarine	25 g
$\frac{1}{4}$ cup	Skimmed milk	50 ml
2 tbs	Oatmeal, finely ground	10 g
1 tsp	Rum	5 ml

- In a small saucepan, place the carob, margarine and milk and stir over a low heat until the margarine is melted. Remove from heat. Add the rum and oatmeal.
- To make the kisses, roll out the pastry fairly thin so that you can cut 32 × 2 in (5 cm) circles.
- Put the circles on a baking sheet and bake in a pre-heated oven (375 deg F/190 deg C) until lightly browned. Leave until cooled.
- When they are cool put $\frac{1}{2}$ tsp of the icing on $\frac{1}{2}$ the cookie bases. Then cover with the other half of the cookies to make a sandwich.
- Decorate with the rest of the icing and a sliver of banana, if desired.

Caroso's Rules for Hand- and Knee-Kissing

The correct method of kissing a hand was set down in 1600 by the Italian, Caroso, in his book *Della Nobilta di Dame*. The kiss is always on the right hand, which should not touch the mouth, being kept 'somewhat distant, and bending it a little, not keeping it straight', and the gesture is accompanied by either a bow or a curtsy. When raising the arm and bringing

17

the hand towards the mouth, with the wrist and hand curving inwards, the index finger (which was often the favourite finger for a ring in Caroso's day) is nearest the mouth. Caroso also mentions the ancient custom of knee-kissing, used at social functions where those of royal or noble blood were present. For instance, when a lord or prince was granted an audience by a king in order to present a petition, he made a very low reverence before the king 'so that his knee almost touches the ground' then pretended to kiss the king's knee, 'and then, raising his face, he will kiss the petition and hand it to the king'. On taking his leave he again went through the motions of 'wishing to kiss his knee'.

Casablanca Comb

We had to include some reference to *Casablanca*. Nevertheless, as we explained in the Preface, part of the aim of this book is to *undermine* the film's suggestion that a kiss is permanent, unvarying and unchanging. So here's something that should be weird enough to subvert the film's paradigm of a kiss: Take a comb and fold paper around it to make a 'kazoo'. Both partners place lips on a side of the comb, so that you are facing each other, lips against the paper. Both hum the first two lines of the tune 'As Time Goes By': 'You must remember this / A kiss is just a kiss'. (Sometimes this lyric is rendered as 'A kiss is *still* a kiss.')This humming against paper may well make your lips experience a peculiar pins-and-needles sensation: if it does, all the better. Then slide the comb to one side, so that lips come into contact. Now do you believe that a kiss is *just* a kiss?

Cascade

Here's a nice piece of kiss-choreography: rest your chin on the back of your hand. Your partner does the same, so that heads (and hands) are level. Kiss. Then both of you slip your chins off the end of your hands, so that your chins fall onto the *other* hands – you should now both be repeating your opening position, only slightly lower down. Kiss again, and slip chins again. Continue in this way. (You should start from a standing position and go lower and lower, making a cascade of kisses.)

Catching the Crab

More material for kiss-sequences. (See note on **Bewitched** kiss.) You and your partner protrude tongues and move them from side to side, as though they are oars. Move faces closer together and touch tongues. ('Catching the Crab' is a rowing term.)

Caveman Kiss

Another way of grabbing your partner for a kiss: creep up from behind, pretend to club them, and pull hair. Drag them away and kiss.

Chameleon Chin Kiss

Force up your lower lip, so that it covers your upper lip – really push up *hard* with the lower lip, and protrude it as well. You will find that a patch of skin on your chin changes its texture, and then, most importantly, the skin changes colour as the blood drains away. Wait until the colour-change, and then get your partner to kiss the albino-chin.

Charity Kiss

The fairground kissing-booth ('Buy a kiss for $1!') isn't the only way of using a smacker to raise funds for charity. In 1993 MAC, a Canadian-based cosmetics company, created a lipstick called *Viva Glam*, total sales of which were donated to AIDS charities around the world. This raised more than $5.5 million and prompted the launch of Viva Glam II in 1997. Also in 1997, the British-based charity Comic Relief, in conjunction with the Body Shop, took the kissing booth idea onto the street: for £1 you could purchase a kit consisting of a lipstick, a log to record your kissing antics, and 10 stickers – so people could sell kisses to raise money for Comic Relief. So if you are having a fundraising event, don't forget the profit potential of a kiss!

Charlie Brown and Lucy

Hard-core fans of TV shows, rock groups, etc often 'theme' their lives, with everything from their wallpaper to their keyring carrying an image related to the object of their obsession. But why not theme kisses as well? You'll find several examples in this book – and here's one for fans of the comic strip, *Peanuts:* Kissee sticks out tongue. Kisser does a 'run-up', sliding his tongue along kissee's cheek, level with kissee's mouth. But just as kisser is about to reach the kissee's tongue, it is rapidly withdrawn into kissee's mouth. Some kissers never learn!

Chasm, The

The essence of this is confounding your partner's expectations. You are both puckered, and your partner expects to touch his lips against yours – but at the last moment, you open your mouth into a 'chasm' and so his lips meet an unexpected empty space. It's a twist in the tale.

Cheng Jiang

Kissing can also be a method of mouth-massage; indeed, your partner's face is a map of Chinese acupressure massage points, to which you can apply your lips. *Cheng Jiang* is one such point, located midway between the lower lip and the top of the chin. Apply your tongue or lips to this point on your partner and massage in small, clockwise circles.

Chess Knight

There's a kiss for everyone – including chess players. Simply travel around your partner's face with your kisses grouped in threes, like the movement of a chess knight: two horizontal kisses followed by one vertical kiss, or two vertical kisses followed by one horizontal kiss.

Chic 'n' Cheeky

Place your lips on the ridge of your partner's cheekbone. Nibble the flesh gently, pulling on the skin using only your lips – no teeth. Do this when the cheek is relaxed, then get your partner to grimace: the two situations give completely different feelings for both nibbler and nibblee.

Chinese Kiss

This is the Chinese equivalent of the kiss: touch your partner's face with a finger and then sniff the air inquisitively.

Chinook

When kiss-fascination strikes you, you became interested in *all* the phenomena associated with linking lips, including the noise of a kiss, and the possibility of varying that noise. So try this out with your partner: both purse lips, put together and both draw in breath. This creates a really windy sound. (You can also try a 'Wet Chinook' – both moisten your lips first, thus creating a moist wind.)

Chocolate Coffee Kiss

- ¾ oz coffee liqueur
- ¾ oz Irish cream liqueur
- 1 splash creme de cocoa (brown)
- 1 splash Grand Marnier
- 1½ oz chocolate syrup
- Hot coffee

Pour liqueurs and syrup into coffee-glass and fill with coffee. Top with whipped cream.

Chocolate Kiss Cookies

2½ cups	All-purpose flour	625 ml
1 tsp	Baking soda	4 ml
1 tsp	Salt	4 ml
¼ tsp	Cinnamon	1 ml
1 cup	Butter, softened	250 ml

1 cup	Brown sugar, packed	250 ml
1 cup	White sugar	250 ml
Two	Eggs	Two
2 tsp	Vanilla	10 ml
1 tsp	Almond extract	5 ml
16 oz	Chocolate Kisses/Buttons	750 ml
1½ cups	Chopped pecans, walnuts or almonds	375 ml

- Preheat oven to 375 deg F/190 deg C.
- Combine flour, baking soda, salt and cinnamon; set aside.
- Beat butter and sugars until light. Beat in eggs, vanilla and almond extract. Blend in flour mixture.
- Chop a cup of kisses. Stir into mixture with chopped nuts. Add a cup of whole kisses.
- Drop heaped tbs of the mixture onto an ungreased baking sheet, approx two inches apart. This makes about 46 cookies.
- Bake in hot oven for 8 to 10 minutes. Cool on wire rack.

Christmas Mistletoe

You will probably know about kissing under the mistletoe, but you may not know about these traditions – and you may want to implement them:

Mistletoe not only gives permission for a kiss, but sometimes as many kisses as there are berries on the sprig.

Some people remove a berry after each kiss – and when the berries are gone, there are no more kisses to be had.

It is good luck for a girl if the first man to kiss her under the mistletoe gives her a pair of gloves.

Unless a girl is kissed under the mistletoe at Christmas, it is not thought likely that she will be married during the following twelve months.

Cinema Paradiso

A teenage kissing-tradition, sometimes known as a 'Show Kiss' involves a boy and girl going to a romantic movie – and every time the characters kiss, they kiss too. (Alternatively, keep a video that is specially reserved for recording kisses on TV. When it's full, have a session with your partner, kissing along with the actors.)

Circus Kiss

You wander aimlessly into the living room as you often do, humming or whistling to yourself, perhaps slapping your thighs or chest ... NO YOU DON'T! For a change, hum the familiar circus tune *Entry of the Gladiators*: walk around pre-tending to be a circus performer in the ring of the Big Top – posing, whirling hands around each other, perhaps even doing somersaults – and plant a kiss on your astonished partner at appropriate points in the music.

Clasping Kiss

Like many other *Kama Sutra* kisses, after doing the Clasping Kiss you start to wonder whether you've got hold of a bad translation of the supposed classic text in the arts of love. The Clasping Kiss is simply this: 'When one of them (that is, the lovers) takes both lips of the other between his or her own, it is called "a clasping kiss".' The text does state, though, that a woman only takes this kind of kiss from a man who has no moustache and it further qualifies the Clasping Kiss by stating: '... on the occasion of this kiss, if one of them touches the teeth, tongue and the palate of the other with his or her tongue, it is called the "fighting of the tongue".' You might find this 'unpalatable' – you need quite a long tongue.

Climbing the Ladder of Suck-Excess

Sit down. Begin by kissing 'normally'. Then one person slides lips upwards, so that his/her upper lip is above partner's upper lip. Then partner repeats action. Continue, getting higher and higher – you will probably finish up standing – as you climb the 'ladder'.

Clock Face

You ask, 'What time is it?' The kisser answers by kissing you in the positions of the hands of the clock. (E.g., if the time is 3.05, you receive one kiss on your left cheek, fairly close to your nose, and one kiss on your upper forehead, slightly to the left of centre.) It's interesting to note that in Victorian times there was a variation on the clock theme. A person at a party would stand in front of a mantelpiece and call upon a person of the opposite sex. That person would ask the 'clock' what time it was: the clock would call out any hour he/she wished and would receive that number of kisses.

Coconut Kiss

- 1 oz cream
- $\frac{3}{4}$ oz creme of coconut
- dash of Grenadine
- $1\frac{1}{2}$ oz pineapple juice
- $1\frac{1}{2}$ oz cherry juice

Combine and serve over ice.

Coffee Kisses

Two	Egg whites	Two
$\frac{1}{2}$ cup	Castor sugar	125 ml
$\frac{1}{2}$ cup	Ground almonds	125 ml

For the icing:

1 level tsp	Instant coffee powder	5 ml
1 tbs	Hot water	15 ml
$\frac{1}{3}$ cup	Icing sugar	60 ml

For the filling:

1 level tsp	Instant coffee powder	5 ml
1 tsp	Hot water	5 ml
$\frac{1}{4}$ cup	Butter	60 ml
$\frac{1}{2}$ cup	Icing sugar	125 ml

Oven Temp: Fairly hot – 375 deg F /190 deg C.
This makes 10 – 15 cookies

- Line two baking trays with silicone non-stick paper or rice paper. Whip egg whites until stiff and fold in the sugar and ground almonds. Place teaspoonfuls of this mixture on a baking-tray and bake until the cookies are pale-brown in colour – about 10–15 minutes. Cool on a wire rack.

- While the biscuits are cooking make up the icing by dissolving the coffee in the water and adding enough of this mixture to the sifted icing sugar to give a smooth icing. Use to ice half the biscuits.

- Make the filling by dissolving the coffee in the water and creaming it with the butter and sugar. Use to sandwich the iced biscuits to the plain ones. Place in paper cases.

Combination Lock

This is a good kissing-game. One person holds lips tightly closed and decides upon the combination which will open his/her mouth: this combination is kept secret, and is recorded by holding up fingers behind the back – for instance, the combination might be one turn to the left and five turns to the right, represented by holding up one finger from one hand behind the back, and five from the other. Only if the correct combination is guessed – in this case, by the person's partner swirling their tongue once to the left and five times to the right on the 'locked' mouth – will the lips open and allow the tongue to enter the mouth. If the incorrect combination is chosen, then you can either allow the kisser more guesses at the combination, until he/she gets it right, or you might allow the kissee to *change* the combination (if he/she wants) – which opens up the teasing possibility that the kisser might *never* get the right combination, no matter how many guesses are taken!

Computer Mouse

You are sitting facing each other. Kisser rests his hand on his partner's thigh, and explains that this hand is his 'computer mouse': as he moves his hand, his tongue moves in a corresponding way around the kissee's face. ('You want me to kiss your forehead? Oh, well, I'll have to move my hand higher up your thigh ...')

Confused? You will Be

Some kisses are challenges. Here, the idea sounds simple enough: you place your top lip over your bottom lip, then rapidly swap positions so the bottom lip goes over the top lip. On your own, this is quite easy – and you can build up quite a speed for the changeover. However, try doing this at the same time as your partner, with mouths together – you soon break down in total confusion as to what your lips should be doing.

Contortionist

Start by writing down the names of body-parts on small pieces of paper – thigh, foot, knee, nose, elbow, etc. Write each body-part on two pieces of paper, apart from 'mouth' which is written down on only one piece of paper. Fold each paper, and put into a bowl. Then Person A is nominated as 'mouth' to start the process, and he/she has to apply their mouth to whatever body-part of Person B is chosen at random from the bowl – for example, they might have to apply their mouth to Person B's knee. Then Person B selects two pieces of paper, and – still keeping Person A's mouth on them – they have to make the contact of the body-parts indicated by the papers: for instance, if 'thigh' and 'hand' are drawn, they would have to touch their thigh to Person A's hand. Continue in this way, drawing out two papers at a time, until your bodies become entangled and additional body-part contact is impossible. (You are allowed to do this sitting, standing, or lying – but all the previous body-contacts should still be maintained when you try to implement the next.) Be careful – our first random dip was mouth against foot!

Courtship, Galapagos Islands-style

If, as we have suggested, you and your partner are opening this book at random, and trying out kisses you happen to see, then this kiss should be one of the most memorable. There is a species of albatross which breeds in the Galapagos Islands whose courtship display consists of a number of remarkable behaviour patterns. Try out the following with your partner: sway your heads from side to side with necks extended forwards; inspect the inside of each other's mouth; click your bills – that is your mouths – shut; wrestle with your bills – that is, do lots of heavy kissing; point your heads downwards, then point your heads up to the sky. Repeat as many times as you want.

Cranberry Kiss

- 2 oz cranberry juice
- 1 oz brandy
- 2 oz grapefruit juice
- 2 oz Marsala

Combine the ingredients in a shaker with ice. Strain and pour into a glass. Decorate with fresh cranberries or redcurrants.

Crocodile Fighter

Your partner's mouth should be 'jammed' open by placing a candy, or a potato chip, vertically between their teeth. Then move in, kiss and steal the snack. This is an ideal kiss for a bar or pub – where snacks such as potato chips are often within easy reach.

Crumb of Comfort

If you see your partner eating a cake, or cookies, take a crumb off the plate and place it on your lips, saying, 'I don't want you to waste a crumb ...'

Cuban

No, nothing to do with the Caribbean – this is the method of blowing a kiss used by the actor Cuba Gooding in the movie *Jerry Maguire*. Press two fingers of one hand to your lips, palm side towards you. Then, move the hand rapidly away from your face, turning the fingers so that the palm side is now towards your partner. Repeat straight afterwards with the other hand, and alternate hands in this way as many times as you want. It's also nice if – instead of using this as a blown kiss – you do the Cuban when you are physically close to your partner: after your fingers have left your lips, press them against your partner's lips. The effect is of an endless conveyor belt of kisses, going from your lips to your partner's.

Cuckoo, The

We know from experience that it is possible to distract, and quieten, a noisy four year-old child by getting her to imitate this kiss – the peek-a-boo quality is probably the reason why it appeals to children. The idea is to conceal your mouth behind your palms: the palms are like two doors which open and close – the similarity to a cuckoo clock gives the kiss its name – with the 'hinges' just outside the corners of your lips. Thus, open the doors – showing your lips – make a kiss-sound, and then close the doors immediately afterwards, concealing your lips once again. Repeat as many times as you like.

Cupid's Bow

Ask your partner whether they've heard of this one; when they say 'No', and, with their curiosity aroused, they ask you to demonstrate, they won't be expecting the mischievous finale to this smacker: Kiss your partner's (bow-shaped) upper lip, then say, 'Twang!' to represent the bowstring ... and finally pinch your partner *hard* for the arrow!

Curry Favour

A lover's game, to be played in Indian restaurants – actually, it is similar to the **Splendor in the Grass** kiss. It is based upon the fact that there was no kissing in Indian movies until 1977, when Shashi Kupoor kissed Miss Asia, Zeenat Aman, in the movie *Satyam Shivam Sundaram*. Thus, have a curry with your partner – and make it a rule that whenever one of you whispers '1977!' the other leans across the table for a kiss, perhaps transferring some food from mouth to mouth. Then, as your lips part, you whisper in reply, '1976,' and you return to chewing very chastely ...

Custard Pie

Lick your palm and splat the kissee's face.

Cutlery Kiss

This can be quite sexy: during a meal together, reach over and kiss the end of your partner's fork or spoon. Then ask them to take the imaginary kiss into the mouth: they're 'eating' you.

Cyclops

Like those 'Magic Eye' pictures? Then you might enjoy this
kiss: stare fixedly into each other's eyes and kiss – if you do
this correctly, your partner's eyes should seem to merge
into a single Cyclops eye in the middle of the forehead.

D

Dark Side of the Tongue

Move the underside of your tongue down your partner's cheek. After the first few licks, there should be a noticeable stickiness of the tongue. If you're seriously interested in exploring the potential of a kiss, you should give this a try at least once.

Definition Kiss

Approach your partner and say, 'Did you know that a kiss is the anatomical juxtaposition of two orbicular muscles in a state of contraction?' Kiss and say, 'You do now.' (The definition is by Cary Grant, quoting Dr Henry Gibbons.) Or, approach your partner and say, 'Did you know that a kiss is a prolonged pressing of mouth against mouth with slight intermittent movements?' Kiss and say, 'You do now.' (Quotation from Dr Bronislaw Malinowski in *The Sexual Life of Savages*.) Or, to be *absolutely* clear, approach your partner and say, 'Did you know that a kiss is a refinement of general bodily contact, the instinct to which is irreducible, supplying a case, in the higher levels of physiological psychology, of the meeting and interaction of the two complementary primal impulses, hunger and love.' Kiss and say, 'You do now.' (The definition is from *The Encyclopaedia of Religion and Ethics* [1914] edited by James Hastings.)

Demonstrative Kiss

The *Kama Sutra* says the following: 'When at night at a theatre, or in an assembly of cast men, a man coming up to a woman kisses a finger of her hand if she be standing, or a toe of her foot if she be sitting, or when a woman is shampooing her lover's body, places her face on his thigh (as if she were sleepy) so as to inflame his passion, and kisses his thigh or great toe, it is called a 'demonstrative kiss".' So try this out and say where it comes from.

Dentures Out

Both pull lips over top and bottom teeth like a person with no dentures, then kiss. Another kiss that works well as part of a rapid sequence of different kisses.

Dial 'K' for Kiss

Phone up your partner, say nothing, but make the sound of a kiss – then put the receiver down.

Dicang

Massage parlours may offer plenty of (often dubious) 'extra services' – but do they know about the techniques of kiss-massage? *Dicang* is the name of a Chinese acupressure massage point located above the upper lip, about half an inch from the outside corner of the mouth. (There is a right and left dicang.) Try to massage your partner by applying your lips or tongue to one dicang, and your index finger to the other, making small outward circles at both points. (You may find it difficult to co-ordinate the movement of mouth and finger – but keep trying.) Then swap the position of mouth- and finger- massage.

Did You Know ...?

Approach kissee and say, 'Did you know that the impulse from a kiss travels along the nervous system at an amazing 140 mph, as opposed to a sharp jab on the finger which goes at 25 mph? In fact, the worse the pain, the longer the delay. An injury travels at 2 mph.' Then pinch kissee's bottom, kiss them immediately afterwards and say, 'Which did you feel first?'

Do You Close Your Eyes When You Kiss?

This is an excellent party-piece kiss. Suggest to the kissee that your kisses are so powerful that, once you've kissed him, he won't be able to open his eyes. Get him to look straight ahead; then, he should roll his eyes upwards without raising his head. Get him to keep his eyes in that position and close his eyelids – so that, under the lids, he is still looking towards the ceiling. Plant a kiss. As long as he keeps his eyeballs in the same position under the eyelids, it is physiologically impossible to open his eyes.

Does it or Doesn't it?

In the 1930s, Max Factor invented a kissing-machine to test indelible lipstick because the workers employed for the purpose quickly tired of the job. We had to wait until the 1990s for lipstick technology to finally develop 'kissproof' lipstick – but is it *really* kissproof? Experiment with your partner to see how long it takes to kiss all the lipstick off.

Domino Kiss

Here's a kiss that's stylish, holds the attention, and one that you'll probably want to reprise from time to time. Hold up your hand so that it is vertical, fingers splayed, with the thumb touching your lips. Put your other hand in a similar position, but beyond the first hand, so that there is a slight gap between the little finger of the first hand and the thumb of the second. Kiss your thumb and let this kiss transfer to subsequent fingers, like tumbling dominoes – each of your fingers moves slightly and touches the next finger. The little finger of your second hand should move to transfer the kiss to your partner's lips. (You can also do this kiss as a double-domino, in which your partner holds up his hands as well, so that the kiss is transferred across four hands.)

Donkey's Tail

A simple kissing-game. The kisser closes eyes, sticks out tongue, turns round several times and tries to find the kissee's mouth, as in the game Pin the Tail on the Donkey. To make it extra difficult, the kissee can change position while the kisser is turning.

Doppelgänger

Hold your face about six or seven inches from your partner's mouth and focus your eyes *beyond* their mouth. An optical-illusion doppelgänger mouth should appear. Kiss this doppelgänger.

Dorothy Lamour

Inspired by a scene in the movie *Her Jungle Love* (1938), in which Ray Milland attempts to teach English to a jungle girl (Lamour). Approach your partner when you're wearing a sarong – a towel wrapped around you will do – and say, 'What is this word, "Kiss"?' Your partner should be more than willing to give you the correct definition …

Double-Handed Blow

Simply a blown kiss, doubled: kiss the fingertips of both of your hands at the same time, put palms horizontally, upwards and blow.

Dried Docking

Both of you get your tongues really dry by rubbing them on your hands and forearms. Then touch tongue to tongue – this is a weird sensation. (As a variation, only one person dries the tongue, which is applied to the other person's lips.)

Drill Sergeant

This was originally a Victorian party-amusement, with one gentleman taking the role of drill-sergeant, and the other gentlemen being soldiers – but one man can play both roles, by barking out orders which he follows himself. In the team-game version, the soldiers have fallen-in in front of the sergeant, and each soldier has a lady standing a few inches behind him. The sergeant now drills the troops and gives the following orders: 'Attention!' – 'Take ladies' hands!' – 'Right about face!' – 'Arms around waist!' – 'Make Ready!' (i.e., bring the lady closer) – 'Present!' (i.e., pucker) – 'Fire!' That last order being, of course, the instruction to kiss. In 1854, a writer describing this game said that, 'In the present unsettled state of Europe, and with the defenceless state of our coasts, exercises of this description are laudable, as calculated to encourage a martial and patriotic spirit.'

Dumbo

This is probably the strangest method of bringing your partner close to you: pull her by the ears until her lips meet yours. (This kiss was once performed in a TV sitcom – but the scene had to be re-shot because the kisser accidentally pulled out the kissee's earring!)

Dux Kiss

Take some chewing-gum and re-create an old custom of the young men of Dux in the Sudetenland, Germany. They would chew a type of gum and leave the end hanging out between their teeth as they danced; a girl would be invited to bite the end off – and if she did, she was hooked. If not, the man could look somewhere else for a sweetheart, because:

'If thou likest not my chew
There's no love for me and you'
(Magst du nit mein Mummla
So hast du mi nit lieb)

Dying Bounces

The partners come together and 'bounce' their lips off one another like a ball hitting the ground. They come in again and bounce a second time – but now they bounce a smaller distance apart. The partners continue until the bounce completely dies away and they are left with lips touching.

Edwardian Kissogram

At the turn of the century, there was a craze for sending a postcard with a non-toxic red-painted area to which the addressee was asked to apply her lips: this would act like lipstick – she would then put her lips on a blank area of the card, and mail it back to the sender, complete with a lip-mark. One such card from 1906 bears the following verse:

> Of methods of kissing there are quite a host
> But the latest idea is just kissing by post.
> So if you would grant me the favour of this,
> Just send by return one kissogram kiss.

You could re-create this tradition in modern times by 'crayoning' an area of a postcard in lipstick (you could make the area heart-shaped) beside which is a blank area marked: 'Kiss here'.

Egyptian

Some kisses are simply lip-locking in the context of a pose – kisses which can become humorous rituals in a relationship. For instance: both do a 'hieroglyphic' pose, with elbows bent, right hands high – fingers pointing horizontally forwards in front of you – and left hands low, fingers pointing horizontally backwards behind you. Kiss, then swap positions of arms so that left is forward and right is behind.

Electric Fence

This is a good example of a kissin' 'n' slappin' game. (See also **Perdiddle**.) Kissee opens mouth wide. Kisser moves tongue around inside kissee's mouth, circling ten times, and taking care not to touch any part of kissee's mouth. Every time kisser's tongue touches kissee's mouth, kisser is slapped on the bottom, as an 'electric shock'.

Electric Kissing

In the early years of the twentieth century, there was a craze for electric kissing parties: guests would shuffle around on the carpet of a room until they were charged with electricity – the lights were turned down low, and when they attempted to kiss, sparks would fly between the lips. If you want to try this for yourself, then it works best on a cold, dry night. Also, make certain that neither you nor your partner touch each other after doing the 'carpet shuffle' – and one charged-up person will suffice. Lean over slowly, and when the lips are about $\frac{1}{2}$-inch apart, slow down even more until the spark jumps.

Emergency Kiss

Put on fresh lipstick and kiss a sheet of paper. Cut out the lip impression and seal in a small, polythene bag along with the note: 'Break open and apply to lips only in case of extreme emergency.' Place in your partner's wallet or purse just before they go away on an overnight trip. (Of course, you could do a video version of the Emergency Kiss: camcorder your lips moving towards the camera lens and mail the video to the kissee.)

Endurance Kissing

How long can you hold a kiss without breathing? (Or, both try to suck the air out of each other for as long as possible.) Another version of Endurance Kissing, which tests tongue-swirling staying-power, is this: put your tongue in front of your upper set of teeth, mouth closed, so that there is a bump. Your partner does the same. Now kiss, and at the same time move the bump in a circle in front of your teeth (mouth still closed). Do this very quickly – while your partner does the same. This is extremely tiring – see who has to stop swirling their tongue first.

Enough is Enough

Kiss your fingertips and quickly turn the hand horizontal with the back of your hand uppermost: a good way of saying goodbye after a sustained period of hugs, waves, blown kisses, etc.

Eskimo (with added authenticity)

You and your partner are enjoying an ice-cold drink. Suddenly, you fish out an ice-cube, rub it on your nose, and then rub your nose on your partner's nose! (Actually, Eskimos don't rub noses together as is commonly believed.

They place their noses close together and breathe in and out to exchange breaths.)

Exchange Rate Kiss

If you and your partner come from two different countries, then look up the exchange rate of the day and kiss in the appropriate amounts. Thus if, for example, one British pound exchanges for 2.4 Canadian dollars, then:

1 British Kiss = 2.4 Canadian Kisses

and the British partner would give one kiss, while the Canadian would give 2.4 kisses in return. (To get fractions – in this case 4/10 of a kiss – move your fingers along and cover up what you estimate 6/10 of your lips to be.) You may have problems with this kiss if one of you is Italian.

Executive Stress Kissing-Toy

Here's a way of making a silly, and inexpensive, kissing-gift for your partner. Take the shells from two boiled eggs that you had for breakfast, wash them out, and fill the bottoms of the shells with a heavy material such as putty or plaster of Paris. Glue a table-tennis ball on the broken ends of the eggs, and then paint faces on the balls, and clothing on the egg-shells, representing you and your partner. (Or stick on photographs instead.) Make certain that the lips on each egg's head are prominent. You now have two wobbly toys, that can meet in a kiss.

Eyelash Kiss

Place your cheek against your partner's cheek and attempt to intertwine your eyelashes with your partner's. Some people call this is an amazing, indescribable sensation ... on the other hand, you may think that it just tickles like a spider.

Eyes Got You, Babe

Stare intensely into your partner's eyes and then, at a given moment, bring your lids slowly down for the 'eye kiss' – there is no touching at all. Or, instead of ending on a soulful lowering of the lids, do exaggerated alternate winking of the left and right eyes – really move your cheeks up and down, for a comic kiss. (Or perhaps, do the soulful lid-lowering, but then destroy the mood by making your mouth revolting – aim for the most unkissable mouth of all by, for example, sticking out your lower lip or showing 'horsy' teeth.) A further variation involves the use of a make-up pencil: write 'KISS' on your right eyelid and 'ME' on your left eyelid. Approach your partner with eyes open and lower your lids ...

F

Face to Face

Like the idea of re-enacting a kiss of historical importance? Put your faces side by side, but with your lips touching. Talk away – so that you 'feel' your partner's words on your lips. At some point swivel your faces round for a full kiss. (Inspired by *The Kiss*, a short film made by Thomas Edison in 1896, which was the first known portrayal of a kiss on film.)

Facelift

Kisser puts both hands on kissee's cheeks and pulls the skin back, so that it is taut, then kisses the cheeks.

Falling Into You

Person A lies on his/her back on the floor. Person B comes and stands over A, staring into A's eyes. B falls to his/her knees beside A, stares hungrily for a few more moments and then, in one move, falls forward, supporting him/herself with arms on either side of A's head, and brings his/her head down to kiss A. The trick with this kiss is to give the kissee a fright – will you fall right on them?- and then to immediately allay the fear with a kiss.

False Lip

Cover your upper lip with your tongue, so that you have a 'false' upper lip. (Practise in a mirror to get it right.) Your partner does the same. Kiss.

Featherweight with a Heavyweight KO

Person A stays still. Person B brushes his/her face *very* lightly – as light as a feather – all over A's face. This can be quite a turn-on. Then B finishes off with a full-force smacker applied to A's lips.

Feel the Burn

Approach kissee and say, 'Do you realise that a good kissing session exercises 39 different facial muscles?' Start kissing and count aloud from one to thirty-nine – breaking off to call out the numbers – as if checking off the muscles.

Feeling Horny

Certain snails have a courtship ceremony in which they rub eyestalks together. Re-enact this by sticking up two index fingers, one on each side of your head; your partner does the same and then the two of you rub horns.

Feng Shui Kiss

Feng Shui *is the ancient Chinese discipline of manipulating the invisible and subtle energies of the cosmos to create harmony between man and his environment – in essence, the way you*

46

arrange your room or living space affects your life. Feng Shui *is a complicated theory which would require considerable study to fully understand, but here is a simple kiss inspired by* Feng Shui *principles:* If there is a wall close to your door upon entering, place a mirror on that wall. Make sure the mirror is positioned so that your and your partner's head are fully visible from the mirror – you want to avoid having your heads cut off high or low. Then kiss in front of the mirror. The mirror will help expand your *Chi* energy and improve your opportunities in life.

Fickle Lips

As you become more involved in the subject of kissing, you will probably start to be attracted to minor variations, which nonetheless seem to have a character of their own. Such as: your partner comes in for a romantic kiss ... but at the very last moment, you change the position of your head slightly, and the kiss lands on a different part of your face.

Fig 'N' Kisses Pudding

Sixteen	Fig cookies/biscuits, crumbled	Sixteen
3 cups	Sweet apple sauce	750 ml
Two	Eggs, separated	Two
4 cups	Milk	1 litre
3 tbs	Quick-cooking tapioca	60 ml
$\frac{1}{4}$ tsp	Salt	1 ml
$\frac{1}{2}$ cup	Sugar	125 ml
1 tsp	Vanilla	5 ml
Two	Egg whites	Two
4 tbs	Sugar	80 ml
1 tsp	Vanilla	5ml

- Place apple sauce in pudding dish. Beat egg yolks lightly and combine in saucepan with milk, crumbled fig cookies, tapioca, salt and first measure of sugar. Place over medium heat and stir until milk comes to the boil. Remove from heat at once. Add first measure of vanilla and pour gently over apple sauce.

- Whip egg whites until stiff. Slowly add sugar and vanilla. Place the meringue on top of pudding as 'fluffy kisses'.

- Bake in oven, 350 deg F/180 deg C, until lightly brown.

Fingerkissin' Good!

½ cup	Apple cider	125 ml
3 tbs	Apple butter	45 ml
1 tsp	Lemon rind, grated	5 ml
Six	Chicken breasts, skin removed	Six
½ tsp	Poultry seasoning	2 ml
One	Small onion, sliced thinly	One
One	Small apple, cored and sliced	One
1 tbs	Cornstarch	15 ml
2 tbs	Chopped walnuts, toasted	30 ml
	Apple wedges	
	Sage leaves	

(This recipe is also known as Apple Kissed Chicken)

- Stir first four ingredients together in a bowl, and set aside.

- Sprinkle chicken with seasoning and brown on each side for five minutes in a lightly oiled frying pan. Remove from heat and drain on paper towels.

- Wipe drippings from pan and return the browned chicken to it.

- Pour over cider mixture and top chicken with the onion and apple slices.

- Cover, reduce heat and simmer for 10 minutes or until chicken is tender.

- Remove chicken from frying pan and dissolve the cornstarch in a small amount of water and add to the chicken mixture. Cook until sauce thickens.

- Spoon sauce over the chicken breasts and garnish with the walnuts, apple wedges and a sprig of sage.

Fingertips Kiss

The practice of kissing one's own fingertips is common throughout Europe: you may be familiar with chefs approving of their own cooking in this way, but the fingertips kiss can be used to indicate that anything is 'Ahh, beautiful!' – a woman, a bottle of wine, a fast car, a skilful sports move … anything! You might also use it as a way of blowing a kiss.

Firestarter

A practical joke kiss. In secret, dab some pepper on your tongue and go towards your partner, as though for a romantic kiss. Your partner will be surprised or shocked and they may not enjoy it … in fact, they probably won't! (And if pepper is not your condiment of choice, you could always moisten your lips and dip them in a saucer of salt: stand very still and offer yourself to your partner for a 'Lot's Wife' kiss.)

First Impressions Count

You are going to meet someone on a blind date. Agree on a meeting-place – and also agree that your date will consist *only* of one, single kiss. You will exchange no words – you will simply kiss and then part.

First Time Ever I Saw Your Face

Once in a while, pretend it's the first time you kissed your partner. If possible, go back to the place where the first kiss happened.

First, Second or Third

Another forfeit used in Victorian party-games. A lady makes three gestures behind the back of a gentleman: a tap on the chin, a box on the ear and a kiss. He does not know in which order the gestures are made, but must choose: 'First, second or third?' And whichever he chooses, he gets!

Flick of the Wrist

Kiss your fingers and, keeping your wrist flexible and your forearm vertical, fling the kiss from your fingertips instead of blowing it.

Flipper Kiss

Kiss your hands and then paddle them near your mouth to say goodbye. This was a kiss we observed at London Heathrow Airport.

Forger's Kiss

If you could only choose one kiss from this book to add to your 'kiss-vocabulary', then this would be a very good choice: you'll find it adds great variety to your kissing, while being a very simple idea. It's merely this: if you are walking in the street with your partner and you happen to spot a cinema-, theatre- or advertising- poster featuring a kiss, then stop where you are and copy the pose in the poster!

Forty Lashes

(This is sometimes known as the Butterfly Kiss.) For the ultimate in gentleness, lightly brush your eyelashes against your partner's cheek, or any other part of their body.

Fred and Ginger

This is a stylish way of coming apart from a kiss. Begin by kissing normally, in a standing position. Then, after lips come apart, do a dance turn, to spin your partner away.

French Kiss

- 1 oz vodka
- 1 oz raspberry liqueur
- $\frac{1}{2}$ oz Grand Marnier
- 1 oz whipped cream

Shake and strain. Garnish with fruit. (It's an intriguing fact that *baiser*, French for 'to kiss' also means … well, er, to go all the way. We dare you to impart this information as you serve this cocktail.)

French vs Belgian Cheek Kissing

Demonstrate the difference to your partner: the French kiss on both cheeks, while the Belgians insist on a third kiss, not necessarily on a different cheek. (Some authorities say that it doesn't matter which cheek is offered first, while others say that it has to be the left. Anyway, you can get five kisses out of this demonstration.)

From Here to Eternity

Take a wet towel, put some salt on it to enhance the gritty feel and to give the taste of the sea. Roll around and put a seashell to the ear to complete the atmosphere. (Actually, it's probably funnier if you simply say to your partner, 'Let's recreate the kiss of *From Here to Eternity*' and then simply pick up a cup or glass and hold it to your ears during the kiss – you don't need a seashell to hear the sea.)

From Sucker to Pucker

Put your face very close to your partner's face. Now both of you suck *very* hard on your own lips: this is hard to maintain – little sounds will escape and eventually you will both have to release your lips. When this happens, your two mouths meet in a kiss.

Full Circle

Person A lies down, Person B is on top and kisses Person A at 90 degrees. Person B continues kissing, moving all the way around Person A – the full 360 degrees – with only mouths in contact.

Furrowed Brow

Place your lips and tongue gently on your partner's forehead, while they wrinkle and unwrinkle their brow. As you will discover, this is quite a strange sensation.

G

Gambian Kiss

In Gambia, a man holds the back of a lover's hand against his nose.

Gang Bang

Friends form a circle of faces around you, cheek to cheek. Kiss them all.

Garden of Eden

A much-neglected place for kissing is the Adam's Apple. (Be gentle, though. The most effective aspect of this kiss is the element of surprise.) Or if you want to explore the theme of Eden in greater detail: tie up one person's hands behind his back – the cord represents the serpent. 'Eve' then picks up an apple in her mouth, which she offers to 'Adam', taking a bite as the apple is passed to him. This can be repeated as many times as necessary, passing the apple back and forth between mouths.

Gas Pedal

Control the speed of your partner's kisses by pressing your foot down on his foot: more pressure means more pain for your partner, but more kisses per second for you!

Gene Kelly

If you enjoy ballroom, or modern, dance, then you may also enjoy a choreographed kiss, such as the following: both put hands behind your backs, and walk past each other several times, pausing to stare in each other's eyes on each pass. Then come together, lips meeting in a kiss, but still with hands behind backs. Finally, put your arms round each other's back and walk away, heads together. (Inspired by choreography in the movie *An American in Paris,* starring Gene Kelly.)

Genesis Kiss

Based upon the Book of Genesis: God supposedly delivered the first kiss by breathing the 'Spirit of Life' into Adam. When your partner is asleep, walk over to him in a holier-than-thou manner and breathe on his lips until he awakes.

Ghattitaka

This kiss is from the *Koka Shastra,* a medieval Indian text on love. The woman 'takes her husband's lips and holds them gently with hers, covers his eyes with her hand, and thrusts her tongue a little way into his mouth.'

Gimme Five

Establish the convention with your partner of saying, 'Gimme Five!' but instead of doing a handslap, give your partner five pecks on the cheek.

Give and Take

During the Restoration period, it was the fashion to pull off your glove, and kiss your own hand when you took from, or presented anything to, a 'person of quality', or when you returned anything to them. But the person of quality was not to be kept waiting, so the correct procedure was to hand the object first and kiss your own hand afterwards.

Gladiators

Both take a cotton bud, put in mouth and try to prod partner's mouth. The ultimate is to knock their bud-stick away, so you can then kiss their mouth. (Inspired by the *Gladiators* TV show.) For the full effect, it is best to do this kiss when you are wearing something nice and tight, in Lycra.

Glove Poppet

Put on an extra-thick glove – a fireproof gauntlet would be wonderful – and offer your hand to your partner for kissing. You won't feel a thing ... and that is the point. You will be re-creating a practice carried out a thousand years ago by certain rabbis in the East, who used to wear thick gloves both in summer and winter as a protection against lust: it prevented them from feeling a woman's kiss on the hand, which was then customary on Sabbaths and holy days as a token of respect.

Glow in the Dark

In the 1940s in the USA, novelty neckties were produced which carried a secret luminous message: if you turned off the light, the tie said: 'Will you kiss me in the dark, baby?' Why not re-create this novelty yourself using luminous paint? (This is available at good art supplies stores and some party shops.) You don't have to use your necktie – put the message on a card, or anywhere that takes your fancy.

Glued Shut

Kissee shuts his/her mouth – *tight*. The lips are clamped together and the strain of keeping the mouth shut shows on the kissee's face. The kisser approaches and tries to insert his tongue – but nothing will get that mouth open. (Or will it ...?)

Godiva Peppermint Kiss

- 1½ oz Godiva liqueur
- ½ oz peppermint schnapps

Pour in glass over ice. Stir. Garnish with a sprig of mint.

Gomez Addams

Kiss all along your partner's arm, moving towards the shoulder. Sigh, 'Oh, Morticia ...' Finish with a lingering kiss on the mouth.

Gomuku

Because 'X' represents a kiss, and 'O' a hug, an obvious game to associate with kissing is tic-tac-toe, or noughts and crosses. However, this is a somewhat trivial game in its simplest form – a much better version is *Gomuku*, which is played in Japan. Gomuku is played on a grid of 19 horizontal and vertical lines, with one person using 'X' and the other 'O', taking turns in placing 'X' or 'O' on the intersections of the lines. The first to get five Xs or Os in a straight line is the winner. To make this game more 'interesting', agree that the person who is X is the kisser, and the person who is O is the kissee. (Toss a coin to decide who is which.) Then if X wins, he/she has the right to plant five kisses *anywhere* on O's body. Alternatively, if O wins, he/she has the right to determine where those five kisses may be placed.

Greatly Pressed Kiss

Like the **Nominal Kiss**, this is another 'winner' from the pages of the *Kama Sutra*. It is described as follows: 'The greatly pressed kiss is effected by taking hold of the lower lip between two fingers, and then, after touching it with the tongue, pressing it with great force with the lip.'

Group Grope

Try this game when you and your partner organise a party. One player is blindfolded and placed in the centre of a circle formed by the others. This player spins round a few times, then advances towards a person and has to kiss them on the lips. If he/she guesses the identity of the kissee correctly, then they swap places. If not, then he/she has to keep on kissing unknown lips until a correct guess is made. What makes this game interesting are the questions it will throw up afterwards: how did one player manage to identify *so* many lips? Why was one person kissed for *such* a long time? Why didn't your partner recognise your lips even *once*?

Guidarello Guidarelli

The most kissed statue in the world is of Guidarello Guidarelli, a sixteenth century Italian soldier. At the end of the last century, a rumour circulated that any woman who kissed the statue would marry a fabulous man. Some five million kisses later, Guidarello's mouth is significantly redder than the rest of him. If you can't visit the statue, then get your partner to stand absolutely still and salute, to represent a soldier, while you put on lipstick and plant a kiss that leaves a mark for all eternity ...

Guillotine

Hold up a Jellybaby, or any figure-shaped candy and say, 'Kiss me, or it loses its head!' And place the head between your lips as a threat. You will, of course, take the Jellybaby out during the kiss ... but afterwards, you may be cruel and decapitate it, anyway.

Hair Licker

Put your eyebrow against your partner's lower lip, and move the eyebrow up and down. Your partner will experience a weird sensation of having their lip brushed.

Half a Kiss is Better than None

If you know someone really well, you can get away with 'minimalist kisses'. Approach your partner and make a *very* brief movement of your lips on theirs – the movement is like an extremely brief smile, with no opening of your mouth. (And definitely no tongue.) The kiss lasts just a fraction of a second.

Hand Kissing: Intimacy Level #1

Caroso's Rules represent the 'base level' of hand kissing, as a formal act of courtesy. However you can add degrees of intimacy to the hand kiss. To go to the first level of intimacy, *kneel* before kissing the lady's hand and look longingly into her eyes, conveying the sense that you are completely overwhelmed by her beauty. Also, let your lips *touch* the hand, rather than hovering just above it.

Hand Kissing: Intimacy Level #2

To up the stakes, turn the hand over and gently kiss the *palm*. Then close the lady's hand on the kiss and say something along the lines of: 'Keep this in memory of me.'

Hand Kissing: Intimacy Level #3

This requires much more *chutzpah*. Turn the hand over as before – but this time, *lick* the palm. You're making it pretty obvious that you'd like to get to know the lady much better.

Hand Kissing: Intimacy Level #4

If you want to take suggestiveness to the very limit, then bend over the hand a little so that you can gaze into her eyes, gently spread two of her fingers apart and, using the tip of your tongue, lick between the two fingers, right on the web.

Hand Kissing: Passé Technique

All hand kissing is, to some extent, old-fashioned – but if you would like an archaically 'quaint' technique, then click your heels as you kiss the hand.

Hannibal Lector

This was one of our earliest unusual kisses – and one which we still perform from time to time. To begin, both put upper teeth on lower lip. Draw in breath and make tiny rapid bites on lower lip – think only of fava beans and a fine Chianti. The two parties move closer together and continue the motion.

Hard Bed, Soft Bed

Stick your tongue in your cheek, making a bump, and simultaneously expand your cheeks: you will now have a bump on both sides, but one will be 'hard' (where your tongue is) while the other is 'soft' (where there is merely air.) Then offer your partner a choice of a 'hard bed' or a 'soft bed' on which to lay their kisses.

Heart Throb

Now here's one for show-offs – because this is a kiss that requires quite a bit of practice in front of a mirror. But if you persist, you will find that it is possible to open your lips in such a way that an approximate heart-shaped hole is formed between your lips. (The hole isn't very big – probably less than a centimetre across the top of the heart.) Show the hole to your partner, then throb the pink tip of your tongue behind the hole – so that your 'heart' is 'beating' . Your partner then touches the throbbing heart with the tip of his/her tongue.

Heart-stopper

Buy a lottery scratchcard together and scratch off the numbers slowly, one at a time. If you get a heartstopper (two numbers the same) then give partner a kiss for luck before the next number is revealed.

Heidi Kiss

It is a tradition, among Alpine peasants, to kiss their own hand before receiving a present. So do this when you receive a gift from your partner ... you had better explain to him/her what you're doing, though.

He-Man

Do press-ups over your partner, and kiss on the downstroke. (If you are not fit enough to manage press-ups off the floor, then do it when your partner is sitting on a chair, and lean over them, putting your hands on the chair's backrest.)

Hermaphrodite

Interested in exploring your sexuality? Then have a kiss in which you and your partner imagine that you have changed sex – mentally and, if you want, in mannerisms too.

Hickey Kiss

To give your partner a hickey, gnaw and suck on the same spot of skin again and again. In the *Kama Sutra*, it says: 'The biting which is done by bringing together the teeth and the lips is called 'the coral and the jewel'. The lip is the coral and the teeth are the jewel.' In England, this is called a love-bite.

High Five

We'd love it if this little ritual could catch on in society in general: Person A holds up hand, as if for a 'high five', but instead of slapping it, Person B grabs Person A's hand, brings it to his/her lips and kisses the five fingertips.

Hippo

Both mouths fall open as wide as possible – jaws drop rapidly – and both partners snort at the same time. One open mouth devours the other open mouth. (This might seem a pretty strange thing to do – but, as we have explained in the Preface, the Hippo started off our interest in unusual forms of kissing, and so in a sense, it's the most powerful kiss in the book.)

Hiss-O-Kiss

In the **Lip-O-Suction** kiss, you can get a pop by pulling your lips apart; however, you can also get a faint hiss. When you have sucked the air out of each other's mouth, one person should relax the corner of his/her mouth. There will be an audible hiss as the air rushes in.

Hitchcock-esque

Stand at arm's length. Focus on something *behind* your partner. Then rapidly move your head in and out. Your partner does the same – and your lips touch briefly on the 'in' movement. This is weird!

Hongi

This is a Maori greeting – simply *press* your noses together. (Not a rub, as with Eskimo.) The Hongi is supposed to make two people feel close to each other – it's a much more friendly greeting than a handshake.

Houdini Kiss

One of the best conjuring-kisses. Take a piece of string, about a metre in length, and tie the ends of the string around your wrists. Your partner does the same with a similar piece of string – but before doing it, they cross their string over yours, so that the two of you are now linked together. You tell your partner that they must not break or cut the string, or slip their hands out of the loops around their wrists. Then say, 'I'll keep on kissing you until you escape.' Repeat this line – with appropriate kisses – at intervals, as your partner goes into contortions trying to get away. When they give up, reveal the secret: you take your partner's cord and pass it through a loop around your own wrist. (Passing it under the loop from your body side and not entangling it with your own cord when passing it through.) Pull enough of the cord through for you to slip it over your own hand. You are now free.

Hug 'n' Kiss

In North America, people often put 'OX' at the end of letters to represent hugs and kisses. So, make a pact one evening when you're sitting down watching TV together that you will have a hug and a kiss whenever you hear a word in which the letters 'o' and 'x' come together, e.g. 'fox' or 'oxygen'. Because this is a fairly rare combination of letters, playing this game creates an odd sense of anticipation ... and then desperation ... and finally utter relief when you hear a word like 'box'.

Hugs 'n' Kisses

Ask your partner to draw a circle in the air with their left hand at the same time as they draw an 'X' in the air with their right hand. This is very difficult – only one person in thirty can manage it. If they fail say, 'If you really, really loved me you'd be one of those thirty.'

Human Chair

This will take some practice – the idea is to sit on each other's knee and kiss. You can achieve this in the following way:

- Person A kneels with the left knee resting on the floor
- Person B straddles the right thigh of Person A
- Person B brings their right knee under Person A's bottom

- Person A lifts the left knee off the floor
- Kiss.

Alternatively, you could try intertwining your legs with those of your partner as you both move to a squatting position. Either way, don't blame us if you fall over trying to do this kiss! (Hint: it's a lot easier to do this kiss in a swimming-pool.)

Human Margarita

We've heard of a London pub where this group-kiss is the house speciality: a line of people take tequila shots, followed by a lime from their neighbour's mouth and a lick of salt from their necks.

Hungarian Wedding Kiss

This is a kissing-tradition of Hungarian weddings. (It should really be performed by the bride and the best man, but why not try it out with your partner? After all, he is your 'best man'.) The woman kisses the man lightly upon one cheek and smites him more lightly upon the other cheek. (Of course, there is endless scope for arguing among yourselves as to whether the smite was light enough.)

Hunka, Hunka, Burning Love!

After you've been kissed, shout, 'Call a fireman! Bring a hose! I'm burning up with desire!' Fan your lips rapidly with your hand until your hunk does … something.

I

I Could Kiss You All Over

Cover your partner's entire face with kisses. Leave no part of the skin unkissed! (Include neck, ears, etc.) You can also experiment with different pucker sizes: keep your pucker as small as possible to maximise the number of kisses required to cover the face, or use a gaping mouth to minimise the number.

IOU

If you're a woman or a girl, take the hat off your boyfriend's head and say, 'Did you know that according to Alabama folklore, if you put on a boy's hat, you owe him a kiss?' Then put the hat on and settle your debt.

I'm Coming Out

Everyone should kiss in a cupboard at least once in their life. Try it out at your office party, or simply in your closet at home. (There is a teenage kissing-game called 'Seven Minutes in Heaven' in which the idea is for the two players to go into a closet and find heavenly bliss by spending seven minutes kissing.)

I'm Stuck on You

If you are sticking stamps on envelopes, and your partner is next to you, lick a stamp and then lick your partner's cheek – some of the gum will be on your tongue, and your partner will notice the stickiness. (When we mentioned to someone that this would be included in a book of kisses, the remark was made: 'Do you think people would really want to do that?' Well, *we* did it – we were glad to find a quick and easy way of experiencing a new tongue-texture.)

I've Got You Under my Skin

During a kiss, push your tongue under your partner's upper lip, between their teeth and the flesh of their mouth. This is a slightly shocking tongue movement – you'd better know the kissee fairly well before attempting it.

Ice Maiden

To give your partner an amazingly different kiss-experience, press your lips against an ice-cold drinks can; when your lips are sufficiently cold, press them against your partner's lips.

If You Really, Really, Love Me

Both partners are given the right to interrupt the other partner's favourite TV programme: this right can be exercised just once, but when it is exercised, the TV *must* be

70

turned off for a full one-minute period for a kiss – there are no exceptions, not even to see the last minute of a vital sports contest, or to see the unveiling of the murderer in a gripping Whodunnit. But be careful – if you ruin your partner's favourite viewing, they may well seek revenge.

Illustrated Man, The

We dare you to try this. Both are naked. Take turns to think of words containing the letter 'x': when you have thought of such a word, write it on your partner's body in body-paint or lip-pencil, but instead of writing the 'x', leave a blank in the word and kiss there – e.g., 'Extra' is written as 'E tra', with your lips being planted in the gap. Continue until both your bodies are covered in such words – leave writing in the most intimate places until the end – but keep your faces and hands clean. Then dress, so that all the words are covered by clothing. Go to a public place, such as a bar – only you two will know about the 'tattoos' that cover your bodies. If one of the words that is on your partner's body gets mentioned in conversation, then touch it, through the clothes – so you can deliberately gear the conversation to places you want to touch!

Impossible Kiss, The

Ask your partner how you can put a sheet of newspaper on the floor, so that, when you stand face-to-face on it, you won't be able to kiss. (Cutting up the newspaper is not allowed, nor tying up your partner, nor preventing movement.) Demonstrate the answer – by putting the newspaper in a doorway, with you and your partner on different sides of the door.

In a Perfumed Garden #1

The sixteenth-century Arabian treatise on love *The Perfumed Garden* recommends a kiss which 'provokes the flow of sweet and fresh saliva. It is for the man to bring this about by slightly and softly nibbling his partner's tongue, when her saliva will flow sweet and exquisite, more pleasant than refined honey, and which will not mix with the saliva of her mouth. This manoeuvre will give the man a trembling sensation, which will run all through his body, and is more intoxicating than wine drunk to excess.

'A poet has said:
In kissing her, I have drunk from her mouth
Like a camel that drinks from the redir*
Her embrace and the freshness of her mouth
Give me a languor that goes to my marrow.'

*A *redir* is a natural reservoir in the hot plains, in which rainwater collects.

In a Perfumed Garden #2

Shaykh Nefzawi, the author of *The Perfumed Garden* also recommends a 'sonorous kiss' which is produced 'by the displacement of the saliva, provoked by the suction.' In other words, suck the saliva out of your partner's mouth, making as much noise as possible!

In Private in Public

Suppose you are with your partner in a public place where there are a reasonable number of people around. (E.g., a smallish railway station.) You make the decision that you will *only* kiss when everyone is looking away.

In Sickness and in Health

If someone appears unwilling to be kissed then tell them: 'I'm doing this for your own good', and point out that when you absorb someone else's saliva, you also receive their enzymes, which give you their immunities – as with an antibiotic.

In Your Face

Before you kiss your partner, really 'announce' it: tilt back your head, stick out your tongue, swirl it around three or four times, then bring your head forward to plonk a kiss on your partner's lips.

Incorrect Air Kiss

There are variations on a theme … and there are variations on those variations. So, stand facing each other. Put your left cheek close to your partner's right cheek and kiss the air. Then put your right cheek close to your partner's left cheek and again kiss the air. You could say, 'Mwah!' as you kiss.

Indecent Proposal

Put the following 'moral dilemma' to your partner: 'A stranger offers you £5/$10 for a single kiss. Will you accept?' Your partner can either answer 'Yes' or 'No' (Y/N) , 'Y' being indicated by yawning in your face, 'N' by nibbling your lips. If your partner gives you a nibble, then start increasing the price of the offer, to find out the amount of money that *would* induce them to kiss a stranger. ('Would you do it for £50/$100? What about £100/$200?' You can also play around with other factors in the scenario: what if the offer comes from a man who stinks like a wino? Or what if he's a male model? Or someone of the same sex as your partner, when your partner is straight?)

Indian Love Call

If you go 'Oooooohhhh!' and vibrate your finger up and down in your mouth at the same time, you get the 1950s movie-version of the American Indian war-cry. It's fun to try this as a kiss: you go 'Oooooohhhh!' while your partner moves their tongue either in-and-out or up-and-down in your mouth.

Inflatable Woman

The female partner stands against the male partner with her arms stiff and outstretched, mouth open and lips protruding, and facial expression unchanging in spite of her partner's kisses – and after several kisses, he puts his face against her cheek and makes the sound of air being released from an inflatable. His partner slumps against him – she gradually deflates – but still has her mouth wide open. (You can do this kiss from other positions as well – eg, the male partner stands behind her as she deflates.) If the female partner can do a convincing doll-face, then this can be a highly amusing kiss. And before or after doing the kiss, you may want to pump your honey up – so apply your lips to the air-inlet valve on her face, (or perhaps the valve is on her finger or shoulder?) and make the sound of blowing her up, until she is ready for you!

Instant Bondage

Ask your partner to cross right wrist over left and clasp palms together, interlocking the fingers. They should then bring the hands up between their arms, close to chin, and clasp their nose with both index fingers. Your partner will then be unable to move. Deliver the kiss now that they're in bondage.

International Candy Kisses

There are several sorts of candy which suggest kisses, e.g. Hershey's Kisses, and special seasonal Kisses for Halloween, in North America; the Italian chocolate by Perugina called Bacci (which means 'Kiss'); and, in the UK, the lip-shaped candies called Red Lips and Jelly Lips. There are probably others, too. So, if you go abroad, try to mail a kiss-candy home to your sweetheart. Alternatively, prepare a meal for your partner, and when she asks 'What's for dessert?' say, 'Something simple – a kiss.' And present her with a Bacci bar.(You might also try out a kiss-version of the Mexican tradition of piñata: Take a big paper bag and fill it with kiss-related candies. Draw a pair of big red lips on it. Suspend the bag from the ceiling, blindfold your partner and give them something to hit the bag with, such as a wooden spoon. When the bag breaks, they will be showered with kisses.)

Internet Kiss

Log on to on-line chat and keep pressing 'X' until satisfied … Actually, there is an e-kissing booth on the Internet, in which you can send an e-kiss or pick one up that has been sent to you. Look up: http://www.thekiss.com/ekiss/

Interrupted Cheerleader

In its complete form, you behave as a cheerleader in front of your partner, saying, 'Give me a "K". "K"! Give me an "I". "I"! Give me an "S". "S"! Give me another "S". "S"! And what have you got? KISS!' But, more than likely, your partner will be unable to take the full chant – and the simplest way to shut you up is to plant a kiss on you as soon as you have said, 'Give me a "K"!' (If not sooner.)

Invisible Man meets the Mummy

The cheapest pair of costume-party outfits comes complete with a cheap one-liner. Cover up your faces loosely in white toilet paper, held on with adhesive tape. Then one person, 'The Invisible Man', uncovers and very quickly ducks his head; the 'Mummy' then kisses the empty space, and says, 'Boy, the special effects in this movie are dire ... '

Invitation to Kiss

Whenever you strike a match – for a cigarette, starting a barbecue, lighting a candle, etc. – hold it up for your partner to blow out. Then say, 'You do know, when you blow out the match, it's an invitation to kiss you?'

Jack Becomes Jill, Jill Becomes Jack

Tell your partner the old superstition: 'If you kiss your own elbow, you will change sex.' Your partner will soon realise that it's quite safe to try this out – it is physiologically impossible to kiss your own elbow!

Jack-in-the-Box

Fancy some mischief in a cocktail bar? Take a plastic straw and discreetly fold it up like a concertina. Then hold it between your teeth. Kiss your partner, and transfer the straw to them – they will suddenly find that a whole straw has jack-in-the-boxed in their mouth!

Jailhouse Lick

Stand on one side of a pane of glass, with your partner on the other side. Kiss. Your hands should 'touch'.

Jigsaw Puzzle Kiss

This is a kiss with a certain sentimental 'Ah ...' factor. The kissee puts the index finger of one hand in between two fingers of his other hand. The kisser then puts fresh lipstick on and kisses the kissee's hands so that the lipstick mark spreads over the three fingers. The full lip-mark can then only be seen if the 'jigsaw' is re-assembled.

Judas Kiss

This book wouldn't be complete without a reference to the most famous kiss in history. But *how* to include it? In the end, it became a dramatic vignette, emerging from our hours of practice in front of mirrors:Kiss your partner in front of a mirror. The person with his back to the mirror turns his head round to look in the mirror, pulls a horrible face and then turns around again, all smiles, to kiss once more. But his betrayal has been seen ...

K

Khyoungtha

These people from south-eastern India kiss by applying mouth and nose to cheek and then they inhale.

KISS

This stands for Keep It Simple, Stupid, and is a business catchphrase, originating in the US computer industry, meaning to avoid unnecessary complications. So if someone *is* complicating things, kiss them in the following way. Say: 'K ...'(Kiss.) 'I ...'(Kiss.) 'S ...'(Kiss.) 'S ...'(Kiss.) 'Keep it simple, stupid!' Finish off with a big smacker. (Kissing, of course, may lead to other complications.)

Kiss à La Capuchin

This was a double-forfeit used to 'punish' a lady and gentleman in Victorian party-games. The couple kneel back-to-back and mutually try to kiss each other by turning their heads.

Kiss 'n' Ride

During the 1970s in North America, when wives wanted to use the family car, and they dropped their husbands off at a public transport terminus, the entrance where this happened was known as the *Kiss 'n' Ride Entrance* – it was actually signposted this way. So if you have to drop off, or meet, your partner at a public place with several entrances, make certain that the one you use becomes your Kiss 'n' Ride Entrance – and refer to it in this way afterwards. ('I'll meet you at the Kiss 'n' Ride Entrance.')

Kiss a Fool

Need an excuse to kiss someone? People sometimes say, when they've got an itchy nose, 'Kiss a Fool', and they plant a kiss on the nearest person. (Also, in Alabama, it's a superstition that, if you get a hair in your mouth, you are going to kiss a fool.)

Kiss and Tell # 1

Kiss your partner, phone up a tabloid newspaper, or the radio/ TV station, and tell them! (Don't hold us responsible for the consequences!) Or if you're a coward, dial a friend.

Kiss and Tell #2

- 1 oz vodka
- $\frac{1}{2}$ oz Galliano
- $\frac{1}{4}$ oz dry vermouth
- 1 tsp Blue Curaçao
- 2 oz orange juice
- 1 oz passion fruit juice

Shake with $\frac{3}{4}$ glass of broken ice. Pour unstrained. Garnish with a cherry and an orange slice.

Kiss as a Fashion Statement, The

Look out for any kiss-related clothing and accessories. We've seen a lip-shaped handbag, a pair of black tights covered in red lips, and of course there are plenty of lip-designs on T-shirts. (Let's not forget Rolling Stones items, bearing their distinctive lips-logo.) Buy some kiss-clothing as a gift for your partner – or wear it yourself!

Kiss Charades

This is the same as ordinary charades – that is, one person has to act out the title of a book, movie, song or TV programme, which the other person has to guess – only here, each title has to feature a 'kiss' or something related to kissing. Some suggestions: *Kiss Me Kate, A Kiss Before Dying, The Long Kiss Goodnight.*

Kiss Class

- 1½ oz kirsch
- ½ oz creme de cassis
- 2 oz lemonade

Add to ice-filled glass. Garnish with a cherry on a stick.

Kiss in a Bag

Kisser blows a kiss up in the air. He then 'catches' the kiss in a paper bag by snapping his fingers while holding the bag between the snapping thumb and forefinger – this creates the sound of something invisible being caught in the bag. He then closes up the bag and presents to the kissee.

Kiss in Iberian Stone

One of the earliest depictions of a kiss between a man and a woman is an Iberian stone relief from 400–200 BC, showing kisses in profile from the shoulders up. It was found in Osuna, Spain and is on display at the Madrid National Archaeological Museum. To re-create it, kiss with your heads pressed against any flat surface. (Eg wall, magazine or road … only joking on the last.)

Kiss it Better

A simple conjuring-kiss. One person puts the tip of his left index finger on the joint of the thumb of the same hand, so that a circle is formed. He then extends the index, third and little fingers of the right hand, but turns down the second finger, so that only its lowest joint is showing. The thumb of the left hand is then placed in the gap above the second finger of the right hand, with the index finger of the right hand going through the circle already created by the left hand. Superficially, it now looks as if the thumb is part of the second finger – and if the left hand is moved up and down, the illusion is created of having a *detachable* end to the finger. This person then shows the illusion to his partner, and wails 'Kiss it better!' And sure enough, when the hand is kissed, it is magically restored!

Kiss Me Hardly

Stand face to face. The idea is to *just* touch your lips against your partner's lips – but the touch should be so light that it can hardly be felt at all. There is no body contact, no touching of facial hair – just a single, incredibly light kiss.

Kiss Me!

This is pretty much the most direct chat-up line of all: Simply go up to someone new and say, 'Kiss Me!'

Kiss my Ass

Based upon a Victorian erotic entertainment called *furtling*, or manipulating a finger behind a hole in a piece of paper – the paper showing a drawing of a girl's night-gown or underwear, and the finger creating the illusion of the girl's flesh. In this version, bend the tip of your index finger so that it touches the palm, and with the other hand's index finger and thumb make a circle, which is placed over the bent index finger. If you turn the finger in the circle, you will see an 'ass' shape appear – which you can offer to your partner for kissing.

Kiss My Naughty Bits

In **Kiss My Ass**, we introduced you to the practice of *furtling* – but there is a much ruder kiss which you can do as a follow-up. All you have to do is turn the 'ass' shape about 45 degrees and – whaddyerknow, it's as if you're looking through a hole in the *front* of the nightdress! Offer this for kissing. (Okay, it's bawdy – but historical practices like *furtling* shouldn't be allowed to die, should they?)

Kiss of Death

Love and death, it is said, are the big themes. Is that why, during the middle of a kiss, one of us will suddenly want to 'play dead'? If we're standing up, one of us becomes floppy and falls against the other's chest. There are also sitting-down 'deaths'. And deaths with eyes/mouth open or shut. The important thing is that the dead partner cannot be woken up, no matter how much they are kissed. (Well, that's not quite true. The threat of an *unpleasant* kiss – such as an ultra-slurpy use of the tongue all over the face – tends to have remarkable powers of resurrection ...) Incidentally, kissing a pretend-corpse was once a tradition at wakes for the genuinely dead in German Silesia and Hungary: a person would lie on the floor, pretending to be the deceased, while others would sing and dance around them, and bend over to plant kisses on the face of the 'corpse'.

Kiss of Life

Not a romantic kiss – but the technique is listed here in case you need to save someone's life. (And really, there's nothing more romantic than that.) A person who has stopped breathing will die within minutes unless air is forced into the lungs – as little as three minutes without oxygen can cause brain damage.

- If you suspect someone has stopped breathing you must first clear the air passage: lay them down, place one hand on the forehead and tilt back the head, which opens the windpipe. Use your other hand to lift the chin and clear the tongue from the windpipe.

- To check whether they *have* stopped breathing, listen with your ear close to mouth and nose and watch care-fully for chest movement. Look also for a blue-grey tinge on lips, cheeks and ear lobes.

- If breathing has stopped, it may simply be caused by a blocked air passage – food, vomit or blood may be obstructing it. If there is any obstruction, turn the head to one side and use two fingers to clear the mouth.

- If the casualty does not start to breathe after the air passage has been cleared, begin mouth-to-mouth respiration. Tilt the head back to keep the air passage open, pinch the nose with your thumb and forefinger, seal your lips around the open mouth and blow in two full breaths, making the chest rise. Remove your mouth and watch the chest fall; check the pulse with your finger at the same time. If there is a pulse, resume blowing at a rate of every four to five seconds until the victim starts breathing again.

- It is, however, best to have training in the Kiss of Life.

Kiss of Respect

Used in Arab countries, when a person kisses someone they respect – e.g., a son kissing a father. Give three quick kisses – the first to the cheek, the second to the forehead, and the third to the cheek. (The same cheek as before.)

Kiss of Shame

It was an old superstition that families who were in league with the devil had kissed the devil's bottom, which was known as the 'Kiss of Shame'. If you want to re-create this without dabbling in the black arts, do the **Kiss My Ass** kiss, but make a pointed tail out of a strip of paper and stick above the 'butt'. Your partner should lift the tail and then kiss. (Actually, the witches accused of kissing Satan's backside claimed, in their defence, that all they were doing was kissing a mask attached to the pagan priest's bottom. This could be the theme of a modern-day Halloween costume party: everyone turns up with a mask attached to their bottom, and other guests have to kiss it.) And whilst on the subject of witchcraft, it's worth mentioning the 'Five-Fold

Kiss': this is a secret kiss used by witchcraft adepts – so, with the help of your partner, make a guess at which five parts of the body are kissed!

Kiss of the Easter Island Statues

Both elongate your faces and pull your ear lobes down. Then one person says to the other, 'Give us a kiss' – saying those words with the jaw rigid, so they are enunciated in a 'stony' way. Kiss.

Kiss of the Spiderwoman

Take a fake spider, roll up a newspaper or magazine and hit the spider until you hear a nice 'smack'. Announce to your partner, 'Kiss of the Spiderwoman!' in honour of your victory over the forces of arachnophobia. Alternatively, say to your partner, 'Save me! Save me!' When your partner comes to the rescue, give them a big smack and say, 'My hero!'

Kiss Off Chocolate Pie

For the Filling:

8 oz	Cream cheese, softened	500 g
1 cup	Sugar	250 ml
1 cup	Creamy peanut butter	250 ml
2 tbs	Butter, melted	25 ml
1 cup	Double cream	250 ml
1 tbs	Vanilla extract	15 ml

For the Topping:

4 oz	Semi-sweet chocolate	125 g
2 tbs	Butter	25 ml
2 tbs	Vegetable oil	25 ml
$\frac{1}{8}$ tsp	Vanilla extract	1 ml
	Crushed peanuts	
	White and Dark chocolate shavings	

- Make a nine-inch pie crust from crushed cookies/biscuits and melted butter. Press evenly onto the bottom and sides of a greased pie pan.

- For the filling, whip the cream cheese until fluffy. Slowly mix in the sugar, peanut butter, and melted butter. Whip the cream and vanilla until firm. Blend $\frac{1}{3}$ cup of the whipped cream into the peanut butter mixture. Fold this mixture into the remaining whipped cream until totally blended. Fill the pie shell, smooth the top, and chill in the freezer for at least 20 minutes.

- For the topping, combine all but the nuts and chocolate shavings and melt them in the top of a double boiler until the chocolate melts. Cool slightly. Spread the mixture on the cooled pie, starting from the centre and working out. Chill or freeze until ready to serve.

- Decorate with the nuts and chocolate in the shape of some lips perhaps?

Kiss that Lasts Forever, The

To get the full effect of this kiss, you have to tell the kissee that you are going to perform 'The Kiss that Lasts Forever'. Then the kisser moves the tip of his tongue so that it describes an 'infinity' symbol over the closed mouth of the kissee. (That is, a figure '8' on its side.)

Kiss the Gunner's Daughter

This is historically a punishment used in the Navy – the wrongdoer would receive corporal punishment while bending over the breech of a cannon. So if your partner has been 'naughty', tell them, 'You're going to kiss the gunner's daughter!' Bend them over and give them a mock seeing-to! (You could, of course, kiss it better afterwards.)

Kiss the Mystic Book

Hold a mock-initiation ceremony for a victim: he is shown a 'mystic book' and is told that if he kisses the book three times he will receive the gift of spiritual insight. (Or something of that ilk.) He is then blindfolded and asked to kiss the book once. Then twice. But as he prepares to kiss the book a third time, a saucer of flour is placed on the book, and he gets a mouthful!

Kiss the Rod

And one for the sado-masochists: extend your index finger to your partner's lips, get them to kiss it, then apply that finger in a quick one-finger 'smite' to their cheek.

Kiss the Woman/Man You Love Without Anyone Knowing It

Make this boast at the office Christmas party ... and pull it off by kissing *all* the women/men in the room. (Of course, it's also a sneaky way of getting all those kisses.)

Kissabubble

Both insert a piece of bubblegum before the kiss, and chew to get it soft. During the kiss, try to swap the pieces of gum in your mouths, without tangling them up, and without getting the piece stuck in the mouth from which it came. The aim is to blow a bubble after the kiss, using your partner's gum.

Kiss-A-Peel

Cut the peel from an orange into two sets of pointy teeth-shapes.Wedge one under your top lip and the other under your bottom lip. Keep your mouth shut until a kissing opportunity arises. (So the next time you're having an orange for a snack just remember there is a way to recycle that peel.)

KISSel

Kissel is a Russian dish made from the juice of tart raw berries and thickened with sugar and cornflour. It can be made nearly solid like a jelly or – the favourite way – semi-solid like a hot fruit sauce. In Russia you can buy kissel cubes ready to dissolve in hot water. Here is a recipe for Golden Fruit Kissel.

Four	Golden plums	Four
Four	Apricots	Four
Four	Kumquats, sliced	Four
$\frac{1}{2}$ cup	Sweet white wine	125 ml
$\frac{1}{2}$ cup	Mango, peeled	50 g
2 tsp	Arrowroot	10 ml
$\frac{1}{4}$ cup	Brown sugar, light	50 ml
2 tbs	Amaretto liqueur	25 ml
1 tsp	Sugar (fine)	5 ml
$\frac{1}{4}$ cup	Soured cream	50 ml

- Cut the plums and apricots in halves and remove the stones. Chop the fruit, then place in a small saucepan with the kumquats and wine, bring to the boil, cover and simmer for five minutes. Remove six kumquat slices and reserve for decoration. Cut the mango into small cubes and add to fruit mixture.

- Blend the arrowroot with the sugar and liqueur. Add to the fruit mixture, bring to boil, stirring. Remove from heat and cool. Pour into six small glasses, sprinkle with castor sugar and leave to cool. To serve, beat soured cream and pour over surface. Decorate each with a kumquat slice.

Kisses – The Recipe

1 cup	Butter	250 ml
½ cup	Sugar	125 ml
1 tsp	Vanilla	5 ml
2 cups	Flour	500 ml
14 oz	Hershey's Kisses (chocolate buttons)	440 g
1 cup	Icing sugar	250 ml

- Cream butter and sugar, beating well. Add vanilla and flour and mix well. Chill dough for one hour. Preheat oven to 375 deg F/190 deg C.

- Pinch off a piece of dough. Roll into ball with palms of hands and then flatten. Dough should not be thick.

- Put kiss in centre. Bring dough up, shaping around kiss to cover completely. (This makes about 60 dessert candies.)

- Place onto ungreased cookie sheet 1" apart and bake for 12–15 minutes, until just starting to brown.

- Roll in confectioner's sugar when cool.

Kisses Across

A conjuring kiss. Follow these instructions:

- Before you start, take a piece of paper and draw four Xs on the left-hand half. Make sure the Xs cannot be seen through the paper.

- Hold up the paper with the Xs facing you on the left. Tear it down the middle and turn the right-hand half around casually to show it is blank.

- Put the right-hand piece in front of the left-hand piece, covering the Xs. Turn the pieces over and tear them both in half again.

- Put the right-hand pieces in front of the left-hand ones and turn them over again. Tear them to make the pieces square. Put the right-hand half in front.

- Turn the squares over and deal them in turn into two piles. The pile you deal to first will contain the Xs.

- Ask your partner to pick a pile: whichever pile they pick, get them to cover the one with Xs and give you the other. (If they pick the X-pile, then of course tell them to cover that one; if they choose the non-X pile, then take that pile away and tell them to cover the other. Although your partner appears to make a free choice, you actually make them choose the pile you want.)

- Draw Xs on the pieces you have been given, and then say, 'My kisses are so powerful that even if I destroy these pieces of paper, the kisses will transfer themselves across to your pieces of paper.' Proceed to destroy your pieces and ask your partner to reveal theirs – of course, they have Xs on them, and it will seem as if your kisses have crossed by magic!

Kissin' Cousins

A favourite of ours. Pull your upper jaw down over your bottom lip, so that your upper teeth are on your chin. Your partner does the same. You now look as if you're the product of several generations of in-breeding. Make a little giggling noise, and bring your mouths together. (This kiss is even funnier if your partner acts seductively.)

Kissing and Stripping Musical Game

Both partners have to think of a line from a song that refers to kissing, lips, or the mouth. E.g., 'A cigarette that bears a lipstick's traces' ('These Foolish Things'), 'Save all your kisses for me' ('Save All your Kisses for me'), or 'I was raised by a toothless bearded hag' ('Jumpin' Jack Flash'). Take turns to sing such a line, and after singing give your partner a kiss. If, however, one partner cannot think of a song-line, then he/she has to remove an item of clothing and be kissed on an area of the body that was covered by the clothing. The game then continues with the other partner trying to think of a line from a song again. Continue as far as you dare!

Kissing a Nun

Quite why this is called 'Kissing a Nun' is not clear – unless it is meant to indicate a sister who is cut off from the world – but it was used as a forfeit in Victorian party-games: a lady and a gentleman kiss through the bars of the back of a chair.

Kissing at Dawn

The love-treatise, the *Koka Shastra* remarks: 'Lovers risen from bed seek to have their mistress' soft arms round their neck, and the soles of her feet placed on top of their own feet. This is a special kind of kissing at dawn.' See also **Tree-Climbing Embrace** and **Gas Pedal**.

94

Kissing Bug

There is a North American insect called the Kissing Bug, which bites the lips. Thus, give your partner little nibbles on the lips, pinching the flesh with your incisors.

Kissing Bunch

Kissing under the mistletoe at Christmas became popular in the sixteenth century*. Here's how to make a simple spray: combine eucalyptus, gypsophilia, lavender and hydrangea, add any other seasonal material and the mistletoe. Tie with a bow – now you are ready for your first victim! (*The association of mistletoe with kissing is much earlier, however, dating back to Norse mythology. Baldur, the favourite of the Gods, was killed by Loki with a mistletoe dart – and, as compensation for this injury, the plant was dedicated to Baldur's mother, Frigg, as long as it did not touch earth, Loki's empire. Frigg turned the plant into an emblem of love, and everyone who passed under it received a kiss to show that it was no longer associated with hatred and death.)

Kissing Fable #1

(A Kissing Fable *is similar to a* **Can You Believe It Kiss**, *in that the idea is to kiss your partner, state some factual information about kissing, and kiss again. However, the* Fables *give the opportunity for a more extended 'story' about kissing: they should be read aloud, cuddling up to your partner, and it is permissible for kisses to take place during the reading, not just at the beginning and end.)* The tradition of kissing a bride ultimately descends from an ancient practice in which all the male guests at a wedding were allowed to 'have their way' with the bride before the groom could assume his conjugal rights. (In time, ecclesiastical manuals laid down the strictly enforced law that the nuptial kiss has to be bestowed in church immediately following the bridal benediction – this was a precautionary measure in case some over-enthusiastic kisser reverted to the old tradition.) But in the disease-ridden Middle-Ages, the bride and groom's kiss came to have a special legal significance: if one of the couple died before the kiss then all the wedding-gifts had to be returned.

Kissing Fable #2

A reader of *Woman* (a weekly British magazine for women) complained that her boyfriend insisted on fetching a face-cloth and washing away all her make-up before kissing her good night. She was advised to point out to him that lipstick has antiseptic qualities which could not fail to cut down the germ count in kissing – and the heavy base tends to suffocate the colonies of bacteria transferred when two people kiss.

Kissing Fable #3

You may have heard of the custom of kissing the Pope's toe, but how did this begin? It is said that originally the faithful would kiss the Pope's right hand, but in the eighth century, a passionate woman not only kissed the hand, but *squeezed* it – and the Pope was so horrified that he cut the hand off. It was the hand's loss, and the circumstances surrounding it, that made him offer his foot instead, thereby starting a tradition.

Kissing Fable #4

How did the letter 'X' come to represent a kiss? It has been suggested that it stands for two stylised mouths, > and <, coming together in an X, or a kiss. But the most likely explanation is that when illiterates were required to 'sign' a document with an X, they would kiss the X in order to confirm the veracity of the written statement, just as they kissed the Bible. X was not only simple to draw but also, being a cross, was a sacred symbol, associated with the promise of truth. More romantically, some have seen the X as a most appropriate choice, however it was derived: as a mathematical symbol it may signify nothing at all, or an infinity (of delight), or 'multiply' joy and love. (Though has anyone noticed that X sounds rather like 'ks', as in the word 'box'? And 'ks' inevitably reminds one of the word 'kiss'.)

Kissing Gourami

One of the most obvious lip-variations is to do goldfish 'gulping' and bring your mouths together; to give this kiss a bit more sophistication, you can call it 'Kissing Gourami' – an aquarium fish which has large, backward-curving lips that are used to grasp plants from rocks. (And, in aquariums, they often rub their lips against other fish.)

Kissing in the Clouds

Two	Egg whites, at room temp	Two
Dash	Salt	Dash
$\frac{3}{4}$ cup	Sugar	175 ml
$\frac{1}{2}$ tsp	Almond extract	2 ml
$1\frac{1}{2}$ cups	Flaked Coconut	375 ml
2 cups	Popped popcorn, finely crushed in blender or food-processor	500 ml
1 tbs	All-purpose flour	20 ml
1 tsp	Unsweetened dry cherry-flavour drink mix (opt)	5 ml
16	Chocolate Kisses or Chocolate Buttons	16

- Preheat oven to 300 deg F/160 deg C. Lightly grease a large baking sheet.

- In medium bowl, beat egg whites with salt until soft peaks form. Gradually add sugar, beating continuously, until stiff peaks form.

- By hand, fold in remaining ingredients, except chocolate kisses, until all ingredients are moistened.

- Drop by rounded tablespoons, 2" apart, on baking sheet. (This makes 16 cookies.) Bake at 300 deg F/160 deg C for 7 minutes or until set. Remove from oven and immediately gently press a candy kiss in the centre of each cookie. Return to oven and bake an additional 8 minutes or until golden brown. Cool on cookie sheet for one minute, then remove to wire racks to cool.

Kissing the Blarney Stone

This is a prank you can try out at a drunken gathering. First, you must select a victim – probably the drunkest person present – who is blindfolded and then told that he will be taken to Ireland to kiss the Blarney Stone. He is sat down upon a stool, which is then dragged across the floor – as bumpily as possible – representing a plane taking off. Then, a group of strong men lift the stool into the air, and move all over the room, carrying the victim aloft. He hangs on for dear life, and eventually he comes to a bumpy landing. That is not the end of his troubles, though, for he must now take a jerky ride in a 'horse and carriage' on his stool, which will take him to Blarney Castle. When the stool comes to a halt, one of the other men – preferably someone with a hairy upper arm – rolls up his sleeve, and offers the arm to the victim's lips, telling him that he will now kiss the Blarney Stone. It is then that the blindfold is removed … and the victim sees a man doing up his trousers – he gets the impression that he has kissed a strange man smack on his manhood!

Kiss-Me-Quick Highball

- 2 dashes aromatic bitters
- 1½ oz Pernod
- 4 dashes Curaçao
- soda water

Pour the first three ingredients in a highball glass over cracked ice. Top with soda water and serve.

Kitty Kat Lift

We recommend this one. Gently nip the skin of the nape of your partner's neck – use the same gentleness as a cat lifting her kittens.

Knife in the Back

If you want to tempt fate then get your partner to kiss you by leaning over your shoulder and giving you a peck on the cheek. It's an old superstition that misfortune will come to anyone who is kissed in this way – it is said that such a kiss will be followed by a knife in the back!

Knuckle-duster

An alternative to 'refined' continental hand-kissing. Write 'LOVE' on your knuckles, in the manner of certain thugs. (Or perhaps you're a thug already and don't need to do this.) Make a fist, press it against your partner's lips and move the fist a little from side to side.

K-Plan Diet

Passionate kissing uses up 6.4 calories per minute. So, find out the calorific value of your favourite snack (e.g., one cookie might be 20 calories) then, after you have shared the snack, kiss for the number of minutes required to burn up the snack's calories. Alternatively, agree to kiss for a certain number of minutes, then have a snack as a reward for your work-out.

Ladies who Lunch

This is the infamous air kiss. Go 'Mwah!' as you kiss to the left cheek and 'Mwah!' again as you kiss to the right cheek – but don't actually make contact. (In London, England, there is actually a restaurant/bar called *MWAH MWAH.*) We have also heard of 'Mwah! Mwah!' being replaced by the words 'Kiss! Kiss!' and recently, there has also been increased usage of 'Mwuh! Mwuh!' (Replacing it with 'Mmm! Mmm!' is not yet acceptable – far too intimate for a 'social' kiss, though an interesting alternative for lovers.) You might also simply say 'Mwah! Mwah!' without any kissing motions at all – words speak louder than actions in this case.

Lady and the Tramp

Both eat the same strand of spaghetti … until your mouths come into contact, with a kiss.

Language of the Fan

In bygone times, women at balls would use their fans to make signals to their lovers – there was a whole 'language of the fan'. So make a simple paper fan if you don't have a proper one and press it half-opened against your lips – then tell your partner, 'This means "You may kiss me".'

Let's Make Whoopee

Deliberately 'unromantic' kisses are often amusing. So put your mouth against your partner's cheek or hand and blow an extremely loud raspberry sound. (Hold your lips *loosely* against the skin and splutter.)

Levee Lover

Both stand on the bank of a stream or river and watch your reflections. Both then kiss pebbles and throw them into the water, aiming for the reflections of your mouths. The ripples from the pebbles meet in a kiss.

Lexicon of Love

Every word represents a movement of the lips – and therefore, every word is, in principle, a kiss. So, open a dictionary at random and choose a word: mouth that word silently against your partner's lips. (If you choose a word which is unfamiliar to you, say to your partner, 'My lips have never made this movement before – but they will make it for you, for the very first time.')

Leybard Gift, The

One of the first references to kissing as a form of love and affection was made by Leybard, the sixth century Saint of Tours, France, who noted that he gave his betrothed: 'a ring, a kiss and a pair of shoes'. So why not give your beloved a 'Leybard Gift' of three such items?

Liana Embrace

The medieval Indian love treatise, the *Koka Shastra*, describes a kiss inspired by the liana, a climbing plant to be found in tropical forests. It is described thus: 'When the slender woman mimics the wanton tendril of a climbing plant and lassoes her lover as a liana entangles a tree ... giving little cries of love and pulling down his face for a kiss, this is the liana embrace.'

Lickety-Split

Some people say that for a good kiss, you should start with your lips slightly parted, but not wet. But for variety, why not overturn the advice about moisture? Both of you should get your lips well and truly wet before starting: roll your tongue around your lips – show your partner that you're dripping!

Lightning Flash

If you feel that your stomach is about to rumble, do a jagged lightning flash movement across your partner's face with your tongue and then say, 'There's the lightning ...' Wait for the rumble and say, 'And there's the thunder.'

Link Up

A gesture made by placing together the tips of the thumb and first finger of the left hand, forming a circle, is known as 'The Kissing of the Thumb and Finger'. In classic times, it was a sign of marriage, mentioned by St Jerome, Apuleis and Rabelais. It is the inspiration for this kiss: to emphasize their commitment to each other, both partners should do the gesture, but linked up, as though forming links of a chain, and then the partners should kiss twice, with their lips meeting in one thumb-and-finger circle, and then in the other.

Lip-Lock

Push your lower lip to the left with your finger – move it much more than you can by muscle-power alone – then bring your upper lip down to lock it in place. Your partner does the same on his/her right side. Bring the two 'locked' bulges together, then gradually release your upper lips, so that both of your mouths slide back to the normal position.

Lip-O-Suction

Suck the air out of each other's mouth during a kiss – if you practise, you should be able to create a vacuum. Then separate with a pop.

Lippy Reduction

Men: go up to a woman and say, 'I prefer a girl who does not wear too much lipstick ... let me remove some of yours.' Be prepared to duck, because you might make body-contact, but *not* with the part you hoped for.

Lippy Trick

This is a fascinating kiss, involving a strange psychological phenomenon: Put out your tongue a little way so that it rests on your lower lip. Now, if you adjust the tongue's position slightly while watching yourself in a mirror, there comes a point where it seems to your brain that your tongue is really your lower lip – try it! Your whole mouth seems to be defined by top lip and tongue. Get your partner to do the same – then bring your 'false' mouths together for a kiss. (If you watch your partner, the illusion works in profile, as well as from the front).

Lips So Clean they Squeak

Practise making a squeaky noise on the back of your hand by applying the lips: press your lips together and suck hard. You can attain quite a volume! When you have mastered the technique, do it on your partner's lips.

Lipstick on Your Collar

Unbutton your partner's collar, and kiss inside, leaving a lipstick mark that no one will see. Sing 'Lipstick on your Collar' – 'Shame on You ...' Then button up to keep the shame a secret.

Liptease

The idea is to make a lip-mark on your partner's skin – say, the back of their hand – but to do it a fraction at a time. Let them see you apply lipstick to one corner of your lips, then print that corner. Then do the same for the next bit of your lips, and print that as near as possible to the first mark. Continue until you have done the whole lips. This can be quite sexy, as your partner anticipates the next bit to be printed.

Little Dab Will Do Ya?

Kiss your fingertips and wipe them briefly down the kissee's cheek.(This is one of the simplest of all kisses, and it is a very good way of finishing off a farewell hug and kiss: since it can be done at arm's length, it represents going for just one more kiss – the last possible kiss – before the two of you must part.)

Long and Winding Road

Suppose you have met someone new. In the course of the conversation, you say, 'Have you ever had a Long and Winding Road Kiss?' Explain that it's a kiss which starts on the mouth, takes the longest route away from the mouth, and returns to the mouth again. And then – if you're bold enough – ask for permission to use your finger to trace out the route on their body. (The route is: the mouth, above lip, along nose, forehead, top of head, back of head, down neck, back, back of thigh, calf, under foot, instep, front of thigh, up chest, up neck and finally, the mouth again.) If you gain permission to touch the person through the clothes, then pretty soon your mouth may be doing it for real!

Looming Peril, The

Slowly approach each other, as if about to kiss 'normally'. However, one person's mouth also gets slowly larger as you come together, until fully open, and his/her eyes stare madly. (If you do this right, with your partner's mouth 'looming', it as though you have found yourself kissing a monster.)

Love Potion

The little channel directly above the lips is called the 'philtrum', which means 'love potion' in Latin. This leads to the following kiss: the kisser sips a small amount of wine, and keeps it in his mouth; the kissee lies flat and kisser deposits one drop of the wine from his mouth onto the kissee's philtrum; the kissee then straightens up, and the wine rolls into the mouth.

Lovers' Kiss

- $\frac{1}{2}$ oz amaretto
- $\frac{1}{2}$ oz cherry brandy
- $\frac{1}{2}$ oz creme de cacao (brown)
- 1 oz cream

Stir and shake together all ingredients with ice, strain into glass and serve with whipped cream on top.

Loving Cup

If you are sharing a drink with your partner, and are drinking from transparent glasses, then press your lips against
the glass about half-way down and make kiss-movements
and sounds: your mouth will be magnified – which looks
very strange when the rest of your face remains normal
size.

M

Machine Gun Lips

Have you really explored the full potential of your lips? Have you, for instance, tried the kiss in which both partners produce the sound that kids make when they're pretending to fire a machine-gun? When the two of you put your lips together the air-stream that creates the machine-gun also produces a pulsing of the lips that could not be brought about by muscular action.

Magical-Telepathic-Hieroglyphic-Body-Parts Counting Game

Try this trick on your partner: Begin by drawing nine simple little sketches of body-parts and arrange them in a circle – e.g., you might draw (moving clockwise from the top): eye, nose, hand, foot, ear, leg, lips, eyebrows, arm. However, make certain that the lips are in the seventh position. Then, draw four small arrows within the circle, each arrow pointing to the next, with the fourth arrow pointing towards the third body-part. (Which, in the example given, is the hand.) Make the first arrow bolder than the rest, so that it is an obvious starting-point. Now, ask your partner to choose a number between ten and fifty, but they shouldn't tell you what the number is. Then, starting on the bold arrow, ask them to count up to the number, moving anti-clockwise – but once they have moved from the arrows to the hand (that is, when they have reached the number five) the arrows are to be ignored, and they just move around the circle. When they reach the chosen number, they should start counting up to the number again, only this time moving clockwise, and starting on the body-part that they have just finished on. (And ignoring the arrows again.) They should not let you see them doing the counting. Then you put your hand to your head and say, 'I think you have ended up on the lips – can I have a kiss for correct telepathy?' (What you don't say is that they will always end up on the lips, no matter what number was chosen.)

Mailman Kiss

Take a Loveheart candy with your favourite message, place on your tongue and approach kissee. Show them the message, kiss and transfer (deliver) the loveheart to their mouth.

Makeover Makeout

If you are sitting reading a magazine and you see a life-size head-and-shoulders photo, then tear out the page, poke two holes with a pen through the eyes, and also make a hole through the lips. Then hold the page over your face, with your tongue sticking through the photo's mouth. Approach your partner for a kiss. (It's more effective if you do this very quickly – tear out the page, instantly make the holes, and present yourself to your partner.)

Making a Meal of It

1 lb	Grated Swiss cheese	500 g
	(combination Emmenthal and Gruyère)	
2 tbs	Flour	25 ml
$\frac{1}{4}$ tsp	Salt	2 ml
pinch	Cayenne pepper	pinch
pinch	Ground nutmeg	pinch
One	Garlic clove	One
1 cup	Dry white wine	250 ml
2 tbs	Kirsch	25 ml
	Bread cubes	
	Selection of bite-sized vegetables	

- In a bowl combine cheese, flour, salt, cayenne and nutmeg, toss well.

- Rub garlic halves over the inside of fondue pot or heavy saucepan. Discard garlic. Pour in wine and slowly bring to boil over medium heat. Stir in cheese mixture by small handfuls, letting each portion melt before adding more. Cook, stirring constantly, until very hot and smooth. Stir in kirsch; keep warm over low heat until ready to serve.

- Serve with a selection of bread and vegetables and a long fork for each guest.

You may be wondering what the kiss-significance of fondue is: the old custom is that if you accidentally lose the bread into the cheese from the end of your fork then, if you're male, you have to buy a round of drinks for the table, but if you're female, you have to kiss everybody, to make everyone 'fond o'u'!

Making Babies

If you and your partner are trying for a child, you could always quote the old Barcelona saying beforehand: 'A kiss on the mouth is equal to half a child.' And then kiss your partner twice!

Malay Kiss

Charles Darwin described seeing a Malay kiss, which is similar to Eskimo nose-kissing, except that the kisser places his/her nose at *right angles* to the kissee's nose, and then rubs it, for a kiss that lasts no longer than a handshake. (And note that there are two ways of getting a right angle – you can either place the nostrils, or the tip of the nose, against the side of another nose.)

Maltese Kiss

There is a Maltese proverb that kisses are like almonds. (Which perhaps explains why a lot of cocktails called 'Kiss' contain almond-flavoured amaretto, and why at weddings the favours often include sugared almonds.) Thus, send your partner an envelope containing a couple of almonds: if they have bought this book, they'll know what it means. (Otherwise, enclose a note stating the proverb.)

Maple Kiss

1 cup	Light brown sugar	250 ml
½ cup	Granulated sugar	125 ml
½ cup	Evaporated milk	125 ml
¼ cup	Light corn syrup/maple syrup	50 ml
1 tbs	Butter	20 ml
1 tsp	Maple flavouring	5 ml
1½ cups	Chopped walnuts	375 ml

• In a large saucepan over a very low heat, heat sugars, milk and corn syrup to boiling, stirring constantly. Set sugar thermometer in place and continue cooking, stirring constantly until temperature reaches 235 deg. F/113 deg C. This takes about 30 minutes.

- Remove mixture from heat.

- With a spoon beat in butter, flavouring and nuts into mixture. Drop teaspoonfuls of mixture onto waxed paper.

- Cool on wire racks.

Mark of Zorro

Kisser assumes swordfighting pose. Kissee keeps lips shut to make a wall. Then kisser makes a quick 'Z' with his tongue on the wall.

Matchbox Challenge

This is an old playground trick ... which your partner may still fall for. Approach your partner and say, 'How do you kiss a matchbox inside and out without opening it?' If your partner doesn't know, kiss the matchbox indoors then run to the nearest open window or door, stick your head out and kiss the matchbox outdoors. Then say, 'I've kissed the matchbox inside and out – can I have a kiss as a reward?'

Maximum Kiss

The idea is that one, or both, of you has to cross as many parts of their body as possible – that is, maximising the Xs. Thus: cross your legs, cross your arms across your chest, cross your first and second fingers of both hands, make a cross with your thumbs ... and last, but not least, cross your eyes! Then kiss. (Of course, women might have the extra advantage of wearing 'the bra that crosses your heart'. Men may have Y-fronts ... oh, if only they made X-fronts!)

Ménage à Trois pour Deux

Person A stands with back to Person B. Person A pretends to be kissing someone by running his hands over his own back and shoulders as if another person were hugging him. Person B then comes up behind and joins in the 'hug', kissing the back of Person A's neck, thereby forming a 'threesome'.

Message in a Bottle

Stand with your partner on the cliffs, or at least in front of the sea. Write on a sheet of paper, 'This is our kiss to the world.' Mark it with the lipstick-print of your lips, and put your names and addresses on the sheet. The note should also ask anyone who sees the paper to get in touch with you. Then seal the paper in a bottle and throw it into the sea.

Middle Eastern Kiss

Each in turn places their head, face downwards, upon the other's left shoulder – 'falling on the neck' – and afterwards kisses them upon the right cheek, and then reverses the action, by placing the head upon the other's right shoulder and kissing upon the left cheek. A variation on this is: a man places his right hand on his friend's left shoulder and kisses the right cheek, and then lays his left hand on his right shoulder and kisses the left cheek. And a further variation: The kisser lays his right hand under the head of his friend and supports it while he kisses it.

Minefield

The kissee thinks of a particular part of his/her face, and draws a quick picture indicating where this area is. (The picture is merely proof of where the area is – and is not shown to the kisser. Indeed, if you trust each other, it doesn't have to be drawn at all.) The kisser then kisses all over the kissee's face … and if the area is kissed, the 'mine' explodes: the kissee does a big surprise gulping kiss on the kisser's face, frightening the life out of him/her.

Mini-Mouth, Mighty-Mouth

Both go from the smallest, tightest, pucker to the widest mouth possible during the kissing – do it fast, and synchronise so that your mouths are either both small or both large.

Miss Piggy

Kisser flicks her hair, says 'Kermy, kissy, kissy ...' and grabs partner for a kiss. Another kiss that's ideal for a 'quick-change artist' sequence of kisses.

Mistral

Breathe warmly onto the back of your partner's neck so as to prepare the ground for a kiss. Then give that place a kiss and a nibble. Goosebumpy!

Mitakuku

This is a Polynesian kiss, which involves biting off hairs from your partner's eyebrows. (If you feel a bit queasy about biting off your partner's eyebrows, then why not pull out some of their forearm hairs with your teeth?) Similar to Mitakuku – but more extreme – is the kiss used in the Trobriand Islands: the unique thing about this is that you are supposed to bite off your partner's *eyelashes*!

Moaning Mona

It's probably best to do this as a send-up: during a kiss, give little moans, whimpers, sighs and cries to let your partner know about the emotions being awakened inside you – you're all a-quiver!

Mommie Dearest

(Inspired by Joan Crawford.) Put on big red lips, open up a wire coathanger to form a rectangle and 'lasso' your victim.

Monkeying Around Puzzle

Find a postcard showing a kiss (for example, Gustaf Klimt's painting *The Kiss*; Robert Doisneau's photograph *Le Baiser de l'Hotel de Ville*; or Alfred Eisenstaedt's photograph *V-J Day*.) Cut it into pieces to make a jigsaw puzzle, put it in an envelope, and mail to your lover.

Monogram Kiss

A fine way of saying, 'I am yours,' and 'You are mine.' Both of you should 'write' your initials on your partner's mouth with your tongue. Put the letters of your initials on top of each other, like a monogram.

Moonwalk Hand Kiss

'Moonwalk' your fingers along your partner's arm – the technique is to slide the fingers back while walking them forward. Your partner then kisses your hand and you make a high-pitched 'Oohh!' sound.

Moroccan Kiss

In Morocco, equals salute each other by joining their hands with a quick motion, separating them immediately, then each kisses their own hand. (We also quite like the Moroccan custom of decorating the right palm and finger-tips with an intricate pattern in henna – why not put a pattern on your own hand in pen and press it to your partner's lips? Note, though, that it must be the *right* hand – in Arab countries the left hand is only used for wiping the bottom.)

Morse Code Kiss

Little pecks for dots, full tonguing for dash. If you don't
know Morse, here's how to say 'I love you':

```
 ..     .-..    ---   ....   .     -.--   ---   ..-
 I       L       O     V     E      Y      O     U
```

Mouth Interior Kiss

The *Kama Sutra* lists the interior of the mouth as a place to
kiss. However, you may have to hold your cheek back with
a finger to allow your partner to do this ... which doesn't
look too appetising, it has to be said.

Mr Potato Head

The kissee puts his fingers up to his face, covering various
features in turn: two fingers over his eyebrows; forefingers
and thumbs as rings around his eyes; one hooked finger
beside his nose; hands over his ears; two fingers above his
mouth for a moustache; thumb and forefinger in a ring
around his mouth. As he does this, he says to his partner,
'Kiss my eyebrows ... eyes ... nose ... ears ... moustache ...
and my mouth.' His partner kisses the places where the
fingers are – the idea is to represent stick-on features. But
then, as with the Mr Potato Head toy, you can mix up the
features, so that they're in the wrong place. E.g., the kissee
might say 'Kiss my nose', when his hooked finger is in the
position of his mouth.

Munich Banquet

We think the so-called 'Munich Banquet' is the grossest kiss in the world. The idea is to hold a dinner party at which very fine food and wines are served – but all the food and drink is passed to you via someone else's mouth. The theory is that by the time a mouthful of food has gone down a line of ten or so diners the flavour has been improved by being chewed by your fellow dinner-guests. If you really want to do this kiss then each new mouthful has to be started off in a different person's mouth: so move round a circle, taking it in turns to be the first chewer – and then the last person in that circle is the lucky one who can swallow this delectable morsel! (Incidentally, it has been suggested that kissing began thousands of years ago when mothers would chew food into a pap and transfer it from their mouths to their babies' mouths.)

My Heart Rolls My Head

When we came up with this one it led to peals of laughter – perhaps it's the ultimate 'ridiculous' kiss. Kissee lies flat on back with arms outstretched behind head and eyes closed. Kisser lies at right angles to kissee, with head resting on kissee's leg – and he then rolls his head up the kissee's body, so that his mouth comes into contact with kissee's body once every revolution. The kisser chooses different starting positions for his head and mouth – the ultimate aim is for his lips to roll into contact with the kissee's lips. As a variation, you can also make a target 'X' on the kissee's body with lipstick, which the kisser can aim for.

New Centurion, The

Approach the person you want to kiss and say, 'I just want to test whether you've been drinking'. This is based upon the fact that Romans are said to have invented kissing on the lips: men returning home would kiss their wives to see if they had been boozing.

New Guinea Kiss

Rub the point of your chin against your partner's cheekbone.

Nibbling the Ham Sandwich

Person A reveals both upper and lower rows of teeth, with tongue showing as a thin 'slice' between the rows as the sandwich filling. Person B now kisses A's tongue.

Nimitaka

The medieval Indian love treatise, the *Koka Shastra*, refers to a kiss called 'Nimitaka', in which 'a woman is made by force to set her lips to a man's, but remains looking straight in front of her.' We wouldn't approve of forcing anyone to kiss, but this might be a good one for a consenting couple to *pretend* to perform.

Nine-and-a-half Weeks

Make sure your fridge is stocked with plenty of tasty bite-sized morsels. Blindfold your partner and sit on the floor of the kitchen. Then offer each taste-sensation by kiss-trans-ferral. Continue until full, bored, or distracted by another activity.

Noah's Ark

Buy some pairs of animal-shaped candies. (At a pinch, one pair of animals will suffice.) Wait till it's a rainy day and you're out with your partner. Then put a pair of animals in your mouth, ask your partner to open their mouth, and 'walk' the animals up the tongue, into your partner's mouth. When your partner has chewed and swallowed, move onto the next pair. (Remember – no unicorns!)

Nodding Dogs

The idea is to both move your lips against your partner's lips *solely* by moving your heads – your lips don't make any independent movement at all.

Nominal Kiss

This is found in the *Kama Sutra*, and is a kiss of very little character. It is simply this: 'When a girl only touches the mouth of her lover with her own, but does not herself do anything, it is called the "nominal kiss".' However, if the girl says to her lover first, 'This kiss comes from the *Kama Sutra*', the reputation of that book will itself give the kiss additional 'spice' ... even if her lover thinks afterwards, 'Is that all there is?'

Nosegay

One of us loves this, the other's not so keen – it'll probably be the same with you. The idea is to insert your nose into the orifice of your partner's ear and then 'wiggle it, just a little bit'. (Rotation of the nose-tip is very tingly for the person playing the 'ear' role.)

Nosy Parking ... in Saudi Arabia

Simply kiss the tip of your partner's nose. Not much to this kiss? Ah, but you can then explain that in Saudi Arabia this gesture means 'I am sorry' – it is used after a dispute when one person wishes to apologise to the other.

Notification

Put a Post-it Note on your face somewhere, bearing the words 'KISS ME' and approach the person for whom the message is intended. Alternatively – this might go down well at the office party – put seven Post-it Notes (half-size ones) across the lower half of your face, transforming yourself into 'Salome' for a kiss-version of the Dance of the Seven Veils: ask someone to peel off the notes one-by-one using only his mouth and, when your face is naked, ask him to plant a final, passionate smacker. You might also try a variation on the old practical joke in which a sign saying 'KICK ME' is attached to someone's back without their knowledge: attach a sign saying 'KISS ME' instead.

Nothing Could be Finer ...

According to the folklore of North Carolina, if in talking you accidentally make a rhyme, you should kiss your hand before you speak and you will see your sweetheart before tomorrow night.

Oh, I'd love to ... Not!

If someone asks you out and the thought fills you with horror, then here's how to do the kiss-off: say 'Oh, I'd *love* to ...' with a certain insincerity creeping into your voice; and then, after raising your hand to your lips to blow a kiss, screw up your features, so they get the message.

Ointment Kiss

Kisser kisses cheek of kissee and then 'rubs the kiss into the skin' with a soothing circular massage movement of the fingers.

Olive Oyl's Valentine

'Olive' makes a heart by bringing her elbows together at the same time as she brings her hands together – the top joints of left and right fingers touch opposite her nose. She is kissed through this heart-shaped gap and says, 'Oh, Popeye!' (There is also Popeye's Valentine: 'Popeye' draws his lower lip down to one side, and 'Olive' inserts her tongue there as a replacement for a pipe.)

One Foot in the Grave

If you catch your partner asleep in front of the TV, or nodding off in the movies, etc, kiss them until they awake and say, 'I wanted to catch your dying breath.' (People used to kiss the mouth of the dying – not out of affection, but to catch the departing spirit and preserve it for generations to come: the breath was identified with the life-force, man's spirit or soul.)

One for the Road

Whenever someone leaves for a car journey make sure that you give them a kiss for the road. (A study by an American insurance company in 1996 concluded that men were less likely to have a car accident on the way to work if they were kissed as they set off.) If you kiss goodbye anyway, always have an extra kiss saying, 'And here's one for the road.'

Open and Shut Case

Ever tried this? Both partners open and shut their mouths as fast as possible, making their lips a blur. They bring their mouths together, opening and closing throughout the kiss.

Open and Shut Kiss

Find something which your partner opens and shuts every day, such as a wallet, book, diary, car sun-visor , etc – the important thing is that the chosen object must have two surfaces which come into contact when closed. Then stick two photographs, one of your partner, and one of yourself, inside the object, so that when it is closed, the portraits will kiss.

Order and Chaos

The idea is that you bounce your lips rhythmically off your partner's lips three times. Then, on the fourth, fifth and sixth beats of the rhythm, you go *wild* – make quick, irregular, spontaneous movements of your lips on your partner's lips. Alternate in this way between three beats of 'order' and three beats of 'chaos'.

Out-of-this-World Kiss Riddle

Approach the kissee and say, 'What do the following have in common with a kiss?' Then kiss your partner, and read aloud three or four items of your choice from the following list:

Whales	Rocket	Volcanoes
Mud pots	*Planets, The* (Music)	Surf
Crickets, frogs	Rain	Hyena
Elephant	Birds	Wild dog
Footsteps	Chimpanzee	Fire
Tools	Laughter	Herding sheep
Blacksmith shop	Dogs, domestic	Riveter
Tractor	Sawing	Morse code
Truck	Auto gears	Ships
Baby	Life signs (EEG,EKG)	Jet
Horse and cart	Saturn 5 lift-off	Pulsar
Horse and carriage	Train whistle	Heartbeats

Almost certainly, they will not know. So say, 'Okay, what do those things, and *these* have in common with a kiss?' Kiss your partner and read a few more items from the list … though this will hardly clear up the mystery. Continue in this way. (The answer is that the sound of a kiss, along with the sounds of all the other items on the list, were Sounds of Earth included on a recording sent up on the *Voyager* space probe launched in 1977, as a message to any alien beings which might find the probe.)

Pansy Kiss

No, this is *not* being politically incorrect … an alternative name for the pansy *flower* is 'Kiss Me'. So, if your partner has neglected you recently, or needs a subtle hint, give them a posy of pansies and tell them about the flower's alter ego …

Party Etiquette

The normal rule is that the hostess is kissed by everyone … while the host kisses whom he fancies. You might try reversing sex roles and see how the guests react. (By the way, according to Emily Post, Etiquette Doyenne, in good society ladies do *not* kiss each other when they meet, either at parties or in public.) It's also worthwhile noting the so-called 'Politician's Kiss' which is used by café society host-esses: grasp one hand of the kissee while kissing, so that you can heave the kissee briskly aside if you should spot someone more useful to you over the kissee's shoulder.

Passionless

If you've never done 'Passionless' before, you're in for a treat – this is one of the funniest kisses, and can have you both in a fit of giggles. Assume a 'standard' kissing position, but with no tongue. Both partners keep eyes open and, indeed, roll eyes around to take in details of the room. (You're not in the least bit interested in your partner, so neither of you should move your lips or head during the kissing.) To perfect this kiss, your faces should 'fall' on each other as you kiss – use triple speed to make the final approach – so that there is no gentleness or tenderness as you make contact. (One point that we would make about the Passionless Kiss, however, is that after a while it tends to lose its humour – 'The Passionless has gone out of our relationship.' To revive its power, you might try the 'No Effort Kiss': stare into the distance, display no emotion on your face, and move only you lip muscles, then retract them, for one quick kiss that was hardly worth bothering about!)

Pawn Shop

In England, pawn shops have a traditional sign consisting of three brass balls. So, boys: go with your partner to such a shop just so that you can boast, 'She kissed me underneath the balls.' (If you can't get to such a shop, then an alternative is to play a round of golf – and get your partner to kiss your balls for luck.)

Peanut Butter Kisses

1¾ cups	Flour	425 ml
½ cup	Sugar	125 ml
½ cup	Brown sugar	125 ml
½ cup	Butter	125 ml
½ cup	Peanut butter	125 ml
1 tsp	Baking soda	5 ml
1 tsp	Vanilla	5 ml
½ tsp	Salt	2 ml
One	Egg	One
2 tbs	Milk	40 ml
1 pkg	Chocolate Kisses/Chocolate Buttons, unwrapped	1 pkg

- Cream sugar, butter, egg and vanilla. Add peanut butter and milk, mix well. Add in dry ingredients.

- Drop onto an ungreased cookie sheet by rounded tea-spoonfuls. (This makes about 30 cookies.) Bake at 375 F/ 190 deg C for 10–12 minutes.

- Remove from oven and top each cookie with a kiss while still hot. Tip: if you like chewy cookies replace butter with shortening.

Perdiddle

This is a kissing-game played by some American teenagers. A boy and a girl go out riding in a car. If a car with one light goes by, then if the boy says 'Perdiddle!' first, he can claim a kiss. But if the girl sees the car, and says 'Perdiddle!' first, then she can slap the boy. What's more, a truck-light is good for an extra-long kiss or an extra-powerful slap. (To play this safely, it's a good idea to save up slaps and kisses until afterwards.) In a variation on this game known as Bridge, bridges are used instead of car headlights. This has the effect of increasing the number of kisses and slaps. (We've played this on a London bus at night-time – and occasionally we cheated, with a mere covered walkway counting as a bridge.)

Philemaphobia

If someone rejects your kiss, then say, 'You haven't got philemaphobia have you?' And explain that this means the fear – or intense dislike – of kissing. Suggest that if they kiss you it's cheaper than a visit to a shrink.

Picasso Kisses

This has given us quite a few laughs: One person closes his/her eyes and is given a pen and paper. He/she has to draw two people in profile who are about to kiss. The other person gives the instructions as to which part of the faces to draw, and in what order. (Person 2's nose, Person 1's hair, Person 1's chin etc. Other parts would be: lips, teeth, tongue, forehead, eyes, eyebrows, cheek and neck.) When the portraits are complete, the artist is told to open his/her eyes to behold a masterpiece!

Pictogram Kiss

The following symbols sometimes appear on notes passed across classrooms:

Which means: 'I LONG TO KISS YOU.' So, if you're working in an office with someone you fancy and don't have E-mail ... Incidentally, if you *do* have E-mail, you can use a couple of symbolic representations of a kiss in your communications:

   :-{}   means 'Blowing a kiss'
   (( )):** means 'Hugs and kisses'

(Not forgetting that KOC = Kiss On Cheek; KOL=Kiss On Lips; and *K* = Kiss)

Play by Ear

Put your lips against your partner's ear and gently brush up and down. This is *very* pleasant.

Porn Star

Kisser places her finger in her mouth and begins to lick, suck and – dare we say *fellate* – the finger for as long as necessary. Fluttering of eyes and head movements are recommended for the more advanced. When she is ready, she removes the finger and places it – still dripping with moisture – on her partner's lips.

Portable Blarney Stone

Here's a chat-up routine: Carry around a pebble in your pocket. At the appropriate moment, take it out and spill a drop of Guinness on it (to make it authentically Irish). Rub the Guinness into the pebble. Bend back your neck and kiss the pebble, then start flattering: 'You are the most beautiful girl in the world ...' etc.

Possibly the Most Unromantic Kiss in the World #1

Approach your partner's face, and pull down your lower lip with your finger, exposing the inner lip. Apply your mouth to your partner's face and pull away your finger, so that your lower lip is held down by pressing against the skin. This is a pretty horrible kiss.

Possibly the Most Unromantic Kiss in the World #2

Say to your partner, 'Nibble my eyelashes.' After they have done it, say, 'Are you aware that you have eaten a mouthful of the mites that live on human eyelashes?'

Possibly the World's Worst Chat-up Line for a Kiss

Say to your partner before you kiss them, 'Your lips are cold ... let me warm them up with mine.'

Potable Blarney Stone

And here's another way of kissing the Blarney Stone without travelling to Ireland:

- 2 oz Irish whiskey
- $\frac{1}{2}$ tsp anisette
- $\frac{1}{2}$ tsp Triple Sec
- $\frac{1}{4}$ tsp maraschino
- 1 dash bitters

Shake with ice and strain into a cocktail glass.

Potato Kisses

2/3 cup	Hot mashed potatoes	240 ml
2 tsp	Butter, melted	40 ml
1 lb	Icing sugar, sifted	500 g
$2\frac{1}{2}$ tbs	Cocoa	50 ml
1 tsp	Vanilla	5 ml
dash	Salt	dash
$\frac{1}{2}$ lb	Moist coconut	250 g

- Put hot potatoes through ricer to remove all lumps, then beat in melted butter. Put potatoes in a mixing bowl, add sugar and beat until thoroughly blended. Add cocoa, or melted chocolate which has been cooled, and beat thoroughly. Mix in vanilla, salt and coconut.

- Drop by teaspoons onto waxed paper. Keep the mounds of potato regular in shape and size.

- Place in refrigerator or other cool place for a short time to harden. Hardened candy should be kept in a tightly covered container.

Pressed-A-Digit-Ation

This is a chance to demonstrate your telepathic powers. Ask your partner to kiss one of the fingers of his/her hand, without showing you which finger was kissed – you then say that you can determine which finger it was. Ask your partner to hold the hand in front of him/her, palm down, fingers and thumb spread apart like a starfish. Tell him/her to concentrate intensely on the finger that was kissed – this is very important. You now apply your own forefinger to each of his/her extended fingertips – press down once, firmly but lightly. If your partner is concentrating on the kissed finger, then this should affect the finger's muscles – and the kissed finger should offer much more resistance when you press down. The other four fingers should feel relatively limp by comparison.

Pressure Point

Put your mouths together. One person applies pressure to the other's lips so that the point of strongest pressure travels in a circle round his/her partner's lips. Do this several times then reverse roles.

Princess Leia meets Mr Spock at the Bakery

To be Princess Leia, hold two bread rolls on your ears. To be Spock, cut a pitta bread in half and hold the halves on your ears. Kiss ... or, if you are a bit hungry, feel free to nibble your partner's ears.

Pringle Kiss

Take four 'Pringles', or similar potato snack. Both put two Pringles in the mouth, as protruding 'lips' – they should be positioned so that they resemble the two halves of a duck's bill. Move together, disintegrating the Pringles as you kiss. Eat up the crumbs afterwards. We demonstrated this at another couple's house where, by coincidence, Pringles were present, and they immediately did it themselves … such is the infectiousness of unusual kisses!

Private Lessons

This is a kissing-game played by some American teenagers. One person plays 'the Professor', the other 'the student'. The student kisses the Professor and says, 'Do I pass?' and the Professor says, 'No.' There follows another, more passionate kiss, and the student again says, 'Do I pass?' but the Professor answers, 'No.' This continues, with the kisses becoming more and more passionate, until the Professor smiles and says 'Yes! You have passed your kissing-exam!'

Pulse Kissing

Kissing is supposed to increase the pulse rate – so put a finger on your partner's wrist during a kissing session and check!

Punch and Judy

(Inspired by the English puppet tradition.) Approach your partner with arms stiff and outstretched as though you are both glove puppets. 'Punch' says, 'Kissy, kissy, kissy!' in a squawky voice. There is a kiss. Then 'Judy' says, 'That's the way to do it!'

QBSP

It used to be the Spanish custom to put 'QBSP' at the end of letters, which stands for 'Que Besa Su Pies' or, 'He/she who kisses your feet'. So put QBSP at the end of a letter to your partner and when you are asked what it means, explain and kiss your partner's feet.

Quest Kiss

The idea is to say to your partner, 'You won't get a kiss from me until you do *this*.' Then set them an 'impossible', yet possible, task. E.g., 'Bring me the moon, the sun and the stars', which could be fulfilled by 'mooning' and then bringing copies of newspapers called the *Sun* and the *Star*. Or, 'Bring me heaven and earth', which could be fulfilled by bringing a bag of soil and by making the comment, 'I'm in heaven when I'm with you.' (Other suggestions: 'Slay a dragon' = Buy a toy dragon and cut off the head; or 'Rescue a damsel in distress = Pick me up in your car.')

Quirky 'X' Trick

Show your partner this one. Hold out your left and right index fingers about an inch apart, and two inches above a piece of paper, so that from above they look like an 'X'. Focus on the paper – and the lower finger will appear to be disjointed.

Raspberry Almond Kiss Dessert Pizza

This will make two twelve-inch pizzas:

2	12" Dessert pizza shells, unbaked	Two
3	Egg whites	Three
$\frac{1}{4}$ lb	Almond paste	125 g
8 oz	Raspberry Jam	250 g
3 cups	Raspberries, whole	375 g
1½ cups	Almonds, blanched, slivered and toasted	375 ml
8 oz	Chocolate chips	250 g
	Confectioners' sugar	
	Whipped cream or vanilla ice cream	

- Whip egg whites in mixer with paddle until foamy; add almond paste and cream until smooth. Add raspberry preserves and mix until fully blended. Keep this mixture to one side.

- Top each unbaked pizza shell with ½ cup of the raspberry/egg white mixture, leaving ½ inch border.

- Bake in 400 deg F/200 deg C oven for 7 minutes.

- Remove from oven and top each pizza with half of the whole berries, ¾ cup toasted almonds and ½ cup chocolate chips.

- Return to oven and bake for an additional 7 minutes. Remove and let cool for 15 minutes. Serve warm, dusted with confectioners' sugar and topped with whipped cream or vanilla ice-cream.

Red Carpet Treatment

Wear a red necktie. Roll it up, then let it unroll in front of your partner – get them to kiss up the 'carpet', until they reach your chin and then, finally, your mouth. (If you've got the nerve, you could also approach a stranger, or some-one at a party, who happens to be wearing a red necktie, and kiss up *their* red carpet.)

Red Kiss

- 3 ice cubes, crushed
- 1 oz dry vermouth
- $\frac{1}{2}$ oz gin
- $\frac{1}{2}$ oz cherry brandy

Put the ice cubes into a mixing glass and add the ver-mouth, gin and cherry brandy and stir well. Strain into a cocktail glass and decorate with a cherry and a slice of lemon peel.

Re-enactment of the Kiss that Lost Thomas Saverland his Nose.

Another kiss for the historical re-enactors among you: In 1837, in Great Britain, Thomas Saverland attempted to kiss Caroline Newton in a light-hearted manner. She rejected his advances and bit off part of his nose. Saverland took her to court, but she was acquitted – the judge ruled that when a man kisses a woman against her will she is fully entitled to bite off his nose, if she so pleases. To re-enact this, the man goes in for the kiss, while the woman holds up her hand in front of her, protecting her mouth. She then pretends to bite off the nose with a great chomp, and shows the nose – which is really the tip of her thumb sticking out from between her fingers.

Rhythm Method

Some people find it erotic if you kiss them with a rhythmic pulsing of your lips. Try sucking harder at, say, one second intervals.

Rocky Kiss

Kisser is at the bottom of the stairs. He climbs the stairs to reach the kissee, who is waiting at the top, humming the theme to *Rocky* as he goes. Kisser plants kiss then raises his arms like a champ.

Role-Reversal

Enjoy a kiss in which you both take on the characteristics of your partner: mannerisms, items of clothing, accent, props, etc. Be careful how far you take it – it's a fine line between home truths and a bit of harmless fun!

Rolf the Ganger

One for the historians – it's based upon the actions of Rolf the Ganger, the first Duke of Normandy. When Rolf received the province as a fief from Charles the Simple, he kissed the monarch's feet by lifting them to his mouth as he stood erect.

Roll in the Hay Kiss

Lie on top of one another, lock lips and roll! (You don't need hay to do this.)

Roll of Kisses

One of you holds a camera during a kiss: snap as many shots of your kiss as you can, from unusual angles. (From underneath, over your head, etc).

Rorschach Kiss

Kisser applies lipstick and kisses just above kissee's elbow. Kissee then presses forearm against upper arm to make a 'print' of the lipstick-marks.

Rotting Crone's Kisses

½ lb	Fresh peas in the pod	250g
Dash	Green food colouring	Dash
8oz	Cream cheese, softened	250g
Six	Round crackers, 3" diameter	Six
Six	Pimentos, drained	Six
1 cup	Raisins	250g

- Remove the peas from the pod and set aside in a bowl.
- In another bowl mix food colouring into the softened cream cheese, until the desired colour is reached.
- Spread a large thin oval of cream cheese on each cracker.
- Use scissors to cut the pimentos into upper and lower lip shapes – you'll need one pair for each cracker.
- Place the lips on top of each cracker, surrounding the oval of cream cheese. (This will form your open mouth) Place two rows of peas and raisins (rotten teeth) between each set of lips – and enjoy?

Royal Redondan Hand Kiss

The uninhabited island of Redonda possesses the world's strangest monarchy. In 1493, Columbus was sailing in the Caribbean, when he sighted a tiny rocky island which was covered in seagull droppings. He gave the island the name 'Redonda' but decided not to land. This meant that the island was unclaimed territory – and it remained unclaimed until 1865, when an Irishman landed on the island and proclaimed himself King. The monarchy continues to this very day – and the reigning monarch, King Leo, has graciously submitted the following notice for this book: 'The European court-etiquette of hand-kissing has become embedded in the ceremonial of the Redondan Royal Court, with officials customarily kissing the monarch's hand on appointment to office. This delightful custom can be, as it were, reversed by the monarch, as a delicate compliment to a lady, by taking and kissing the back of her hand, whilst murmuring some flattering compliment. The value of this practice lies in the little-known fact that if the subject's hand, on closer inspection, appears somewhat unsavoury, a sensitive monarch can easily transfer the kiss, at the last moment, to the back of his own hand instead, without spoiling the compliment.'

S & M

Apply a wax strip to a hairy area of your partner's body. Tear off, hear their howls, and then kiss the area. (Do it *especially* if they don't want to be waxed!)

Safe Sex

More kitchen-kissing antics: hold a sheet of Clingfilm in your hands, covering your mouth, as you kiss. (The weird thing about this is that you are aware of the pressure, and movements, of your partner's tongue and lips, but they are stripped of all moisture and taste.)

Sea Lion Kiss

This is pretty dumb, but based upon the fact that sea lions rub mouths. So, clap your hands, make 'Orr Orr' noises and rub mouths together.(You can also try 'Training the Seal': You are sitting opposite each other. Person A kisses both his palms, then puts his elbows on the table with his hands held high, about shoulder-width apart. Person B then chops her hand quickly between Person A's palms – and simultaneously Person A brings his hands together, to try to pass the kiss to Person B's hand. However, it is quite difficult to do this – human reactions just aren't very fast – and Person A just ends up clapping his hands together. After a few more failed attempts, Person B closes his eyes during the chop – and then Person A should be able to transfer the kiss, by anticipating the movement of Person B's hand.)

Sealed with a Kiss

In the days when people sealed letters with wax, a little drop of wax at the side of the seal was known as a kiss. So, buy yourself some sealing wax when you're next going to write to your partner, make a 'kiss' and explain what the drop means inside the letter.

Second Hand Kisses

This was a Victorian party-amusement … but it would be intriguing to revive it in modern times. A woman chooses a female friend, who presents herself to a gentleman, who kisses her. She then carries the kiss back to her companion. This is repeated as many times as there are gentlemen at the party.

Secret Kiss

Actually, this is a *mock* secret kiss, which we observed at a New Year's Eve party. Suppose for some reason you are going to kiss your partner when other people are around: raise one hand as a 'screen' in front of your lips behind which you and your partner can kiss with a modicum of 'privacy'. (In reality, everyone can see what you're doing.)

Send for the Tooth-Fairy

Just before you kiss your partner, conceal in your mouth some mints, or other small white candies which, at first glance, look like teeth. The important thing is not to let your partner know you've done this. Proceed to kiss your partner. Then – either after a forceful tonguing session, or as you bring your mouth against his/hers with a deliberate bump – start coughing. Pull away ... and spit the 'teeth' into your palm for your horrified partner to see.

Seven Dwarfs

Kisser approaches kissee and gives seven kisses, each in the style of one of the Seven Dwarfs: Sleepy, Grumpy, Sneezy, Happy, Doc (ask kissee to say 'Ah'), Bashful (hide your face before and after kiss) and Dopey (move your ears with your fingers and bat your eyelids).

Shock to the System

The tongue is an extremely sensitive detector of electric current. So, if you take a nail, attach it to a copper wire, and put both nail and wire in your mouth, you should be able to detect a faint electric current – you may feel a tingling, or simply a change in the taste in your mouth. Do this during a kiss, with both partners touching the 'electrodes'.

Shoehorn

A bit rough, this one – be careful the kissee doesn't feel 'invaded'. Person A puts a finger in the corner of Person B's mouth, gently pulls back the lip, and slides his tongue in.

Sicilian Kiss

- ½ oz amaretto
- ½ oz Southern Comfort

Mix together and drink as a chaser to beers. (This is also known as a Southern Kiss.)

Sign Language Kiss

American Sign Language uses three alternatives for a kiss: 1) Bend your right hand so that the fingers are horizontal, palm down, with the thumb sticking up beside the fingers – known as the *bent hand* position. Touch the fingertips of that hand first to the right side of the mouth and then to the right cheek. 2) Put both of your hands in the so-called *flattened O* position, in which the thumb touches the finger-tips, but the 'O'-shape formed thereby is squashed. Put both of your hands in front of the chest, right hand somewhat forward of the left, palms facing each other. Bring the finger-tips together – this represents two mouths coming together. 3) Put your right hand in the flattened O position and touch the fingertips of that hand, palm facing down, to the right side of the mouth. Open the hand and lay the palm against the right side of your face. There is also the British Sign Language for a kiss: touch your lips with two fingers (palm towards lips) then turn the fingers outwards and touch two fingers of the other hand. All the sign language kisses could be used as a way of signalling across a crowded room.

Sign of a Real Man

Kisser says: 'How do you know when a real man has kissed you?'
Kissee says: 'Don't know.'
Kisser says: 'Come here, and I'll show you.'

Siren, The

One person creates the loudest, shrillest, most ear-piercing sound they can – like a siren, or car-alarm. (Try going la-la-la very quickly and very high-pitched.) The sound continues until the person is kissed.

Ski Jump

Kisser slides tongue down kissee's nose, 'jumps' into air and lands on kissee's mouth for a final kiss. For added effect, cry out 'Wheeeeeee!' (or a similar exuberant noise) when launching into the air.

Skin Flick

Say to your partner, 'I've got a message for you.' Then lightly scratch 'XXX' with your fingernail on the skin on the inside of your forearm. Don't let your partner see you do this. Show your forearm to your partner – it will seem just like an ordinary, unmarked limb. Then rub the forearm quickly with the palm of your hand – and the 'XXX' will appear magically, as reddened skin.

Slam Dunk

Do a series of little kisses up the chest and neck of your partner (to represent dribbling) and then drop your tongue in their mouth to represent shooting the basket.

Slap Happy

Stand facing each other. Both extend right hand to partner's left cheek. Then bring that hand to touch your own lips for a kiss. Then do the same with the other hand. Keep on alternating in time with your partner. (Dance music can help you get the beat.)

Slow Comfortable Screw up Against the Wall with a Kiss

- $\frac{3}{4}$ oz vodka
- $\frac{1}{2}$ oz sloe gin
- $\frac{1}{2}$ oz Southern Comfort
- orange juice
- amaretto
- Galliano

Mix in a tall glass with ice and fill with orange juice. Add a splash of Galliano, stir and float a splash of amaretto on top for the kiss.

Smoke gets in your Eyes

One person blows a smoke ring low down. As the ring rises, the *theory* is to kiss, with lips meeting in the ring ... but this is difficult, hence the title of this kiss.

Sneaky Snack

(This is one of our favourite kisses ... you might not like the sound of it, but believe us, it can be very funny if you like practical jokes.) You've always wondered what to do with those little bits of food that get stuck in your teeth – well, here's the answer. Work the food loose discreetly, so that your partner doesn't know. Then approach your partner romantically for a kiss – and transfer the food to their mouth. It's pretty gross – but good for a laugh, as your partner just won't be expecting it. (You'd be surprised how many times this works.) You can also try this with larger bits of food – be audacious! And when you have given your partner a few Sneaky Snack experiences, you reach a stage when you can say, 'Do you trust me?' And your partner has to decide whether to risk a kiss – is your mouth empty or not? (A further variation is to show your tongue afterwards with the food still on it – you could have sneaky snacked, but showed mercy, and didn't.)

Social Climber

In ancient times, people of equal social class kissed each other on the cheek, lips or head. Inferiors were never allowed such liberties with superiors: the lower the rank of the kisser, the lower the position on the body the kiss had to be – the lowest kiss of all being kissing the ground in front of your superior's feet. This suggests the Social

Climber kiss, where the kisser kisses the following places on their partner in the following order: ground, foot, hem, knee, hand and then face.

Sofa, The

If you're at a party with your partner, then try to persuade one of the other guests to get down on all fours, resembling a sofa. (You may have to slip them some money as an incentive.) Then you and your partner sit down comfortably on this sofa and kiss.

Solar System Kiss

For hundreds of years, astrologers have associated parts of the face with planetary objects. So, kiss the following parts of your lover's face, naming the celestial body as you go:

Forehead	=	Mars
Right Eye	=	Sun
Left Eye	=	Venus
Right Ear	=	Jupiter
Left Ear	=	Saturn
Nose	=	Moon
Mouth	=	Mercury

(This is based upon the seventeenth-century system of Jean Belot.)

Sonny Gets Kissed

- ½ oz light rum
- ½ oz apricot brandy
- 2 tsp lime juice
- 2 tsp lemon juice
- ½ tsp fine sugar

Combine all ingredients with ice. Shake well and strain into a cocktail glass and serve.

Soul Kiss Cocktail

- ¾ oz dry vermouth
- ¾ oz bourbon
- 1½ tsp Dubonnet
- 1¼ tsp orange juice

Shake all ingredients with ice, strain into cocktail glass and serve.

Speedy Gonzales in Love

Both partners say, 'I love you' alternately. They say it again and again, getting faster and faster. Finally one partner splutters his/her lips – making a sound a bit like saying 'Brrrrr ....' on a cold day – and says, 'That's a load of 'I Love Yous' stuck together.' Then he/she moves in speedily for the final kiss.

Spiralling

Kiss the tip of your finger. Move it in a spiral in front of your partner, centring on the mouth – your partner's eyes will follow it. Just as your fingertip is about to make contact with their lips, tap the back of your hand, to add an element of surprise as the kiss strikes. (But be careful, don't use too much force to hit your hand – or your partner's next stop will be the dentist. Also, don't do this if your fingernail is sharp.)

Spit and Polish

Get close to your partner's cheek or the back of their hand. Spit on it – and very quickly move your mouth onto their flesh and rub the spit in, moving your mouth from side to side. Do this rubbing action so quickly that your partner does not have a chance to be offended by the spitting.

Splendor in the Grass

Before 1961, kissing in Hollywood movies may have *looked* passionate, but the practice was for both actors and actresses to keep their teeth clenched. It was Warren Beatty – why aren't we surprised? – who first defied the convention, when kissing Natalie Wood in the 1961 movie *Splendor in the Grass*. So, first kiss your partner in the old style, acting passionate but keeping teeth firmly clenched, until you feel the urge to change to post-1960-style, with lots of tongue.

Spot Kiss

Keep on staring at a particular point on your partner's face, so that they start to think there is something on their face. When they ask – as they surely will – what you are looking at, say, 'Nothing.' Then when they say, 'Is there something on my face?' reply, 'There's nothing on your face.' Then quickly give them a peck on the spot and say, 'But there is now!'

The Splits

Stand facing your partner. Touch your index and second finger to your own lips and then – parting the fingers like a fork – apply the fingertips to your partner's forehead and draw them slowly down his/her face. Whisper to your partner, 'Close your eyes,' just as the fingers are about to reach the eyelids (if he/she hasn't already closed them) and continue moving downwards. Finish by bringing the fingers together when they reach your partner's mouth. This can be a very sensual kiss if performed slowly and gently.

Squash, The

As your partner kisses you on the cheek, put your hand around their head and press them towards you – really squash them against you. It will make your partner's face tingle for several minutes afterwards.

Stalled Outboard Motor

Both partners blow a stream of air between their lips, so that their mouths vibrate. (Rather like going 'Brrrr ...' on a chilly day.) They then touch lips to 'stall the motor'.

Starlet Kiss

This is a way of blowing a kiss – demonstrated by the likes of Marilyn Monroe. Blow a kiss, bringing both of your hands to your lips, then spread your arms wide and wiggle all the fingers up and down, as though each finger has a kiss on the end and is saying goodbye.

Start Without Me

As a prelude to a kissing-session, sit opposite your partner and begin to kiss yourself: kiss and lick your fingertips, the back of your hand, along your forearm, and anywhere else you can reach. Then invite your partner to join in!

Strawberry Kiss

- 3 oz strawberry puree
- $1\frac{1}{2}$ oz pineapple juice
- $\frac{1}{2}$ oz lemon juice
- $\frac{1}{2}$ oz whipped cream
- $\frac{1}{2}$ tsp castor sugar

Blend briefly with crushed ice and pour into a frosted glass.

Street-sign Named Desire, A

If you find a street- or place-name which contains anything kiss- or mouth-related, then you have to kiss in front of it, trying to cover up the non-kiss part of the name with your bodies. (Eg, cover up the 'ley' in Gumley Gardens, or the 'Ply' in Plymouth Wharf, or the 'C' and 'Stone' in 'Clipstone

Street'.) Don't forget to look for names such as Peckford Place – and foreign words are okay, too. (Such as Boucher Close, containing the French word 'bouche', meaning mouth.) Get a passer-by to take a photograph of your kiss – and try to build up a collection of kiss-sign pictures. (In Cheshire, England, there is actually a place called Kiss Arse Hill – at Rainon – and also Kiss Arse Wood – at Wincle.)

Suck the Life out of Me

In some respects this is a comical kiss – and yet it is not without a certain symbolic importance. Suck some breath from your partner's mouth (puff out your cheeks storing it there.) Next invite them to place their ear on your throat, and you swallow loudly so they can hear their life being swallowed.

Sucky Kissy Face

Person A sucks on Person B's upper lip, while Person B sucks on Person A's lower lip. This is rather like 'Kiss of the Upper Lip' which is mentioned in the *Kama Sutra*: 'When a man kisses the upper lip of a woman, while she in return kisses his lower lip, it is called "The kiss of the upper lip." ' Here, however, simultaneous sucking is involved.

Sugar Lips

The inspiration for this one came while we were looking for Christmas gifts in a kitchenware store and we discovered that it's possible to buy a *lip-shaped* cookie cutter. So hunt around until you find such a cutter and then try out this recipe. (OK, at a pinch and with steady hand, you can cut out a lip shape with a sharp knife.)

156

Sugar Cookies

1 cup	Butter	250 ml
$\frac{1}{2}$ cup	Lightly packed brown sugar	125 ml
$\frac{1}{2}$ cup	White sugar	125 ml
One	Egg	One
$\frac{1}{2}$ tsp	Vanilla	2 ml
2 cups	Flour	500 ml
1tsp	Baking soda	5 ml
1tsp	Cream of tartar	5 ml

- In a large bowl, cream butter. Add brown sugar and granulated sugar, beat until light and fluffy. Beat in egg, then vanilla.

- Sift or stir together flour, baking soda and cream of tartar. Gradually add dry ingredients to creamed mixture, stirring just until blended.

- Divide dough in half, wrap in waxed/greaseproof paper; chill for at least 3 hours.

- Working with 1 portion of dough at a time, roll out to thickness of $\frac{1}{4}$ inch or less. With your *lip* cutter, cut out cookies and transfer to ungreased baking sheets about 1–$1\frac{1}{2}$ inches apart.

- Bake at 375 deg F/190 deg C for 8 minutes or until lightly browned. Cool on wire racks. For that personal touch you could always decorate your lips with a butter icing coloured to the shade of your favourite lipstick.

Suitors

This is an excellent kissing-game, which truly explores the nuances of kissing. Take a pack of cards, shuffle them and deal them out face down to yourself and your partner, so that each of you now has 26 cards. Each card in the pack represents a different level of passion, on a scale of 1–52.

Hearts represent the greatest passion (of course), followed by Diamonds (diamond rings indicate a pretty good relationship), then Clubs (you may meet someone in a club) and finally Spades (your relationship is a dead-loss – you might as well be kissing a corpse, dug up with a spade.) Aces are high, so the Ace of Hearts represents the most passionate card in the entire pack, while the Two of Spades represents the lowest level of passion. Pick up a card from your pile, look at it, and without showing your partner what it is, kiss your partner with a degree of passion appropriate to the card. (And remember, there are 52 degrees of passion.) Your partner then has to try to guess *precisely* which card you picked up from your pile. Take turns to do this, and work your way through the entire pack – see how many cards you and your partner get right.

Summer Breeze

As your lips approach your partner's, try breathing out gently and warmly in the last stages of the approach. This is a nice and soothing way of leading into a kiss.

Swaziland Kiss

A marriage in Swaziland is not deemed valid until there is a public embrace consisting of at least 100 kisses – so 'consummate' your relationship the Swaziland way!

Swiss Bat Kiss

Swiss fruit bats have a mating ritual involving slow head rotations which speed up as the two bodies approach – until the heads are spinning around at an incredible rate. (The whole ritual can last eight hours.) This has led the Swiss to develop what they call a 'bat-kiss'. The idea is to combine clockwise head movement with anti-clockwise tongue movement: an extremely difficult kiss to master.

Swiss Kiss

Hold up a thin slice of Emmenthal or Gruyère and kiss through a hole. Breathe in deeply to get the full cheesy aroma.

Sword Swallower

One person holds their head back and opens mouth wide. The other makes a 'sword', using the index finger of one hand as the blade, and the pinkie of the other hand lying across to form the hilt. The sword is then inserted into the first person's mouth, to the hilt ... be careful they don't gag!

Tacky Kiss

If you open and close your mouth a number of times, firstly the moisture on the lips goes, and then (if you open *slowly*) you will notice that the upper lip starts to adhere to the lower lip. Both of you should reach this stage. Then come together and try to stick your tacky upper lip to your partner's tacky lower lip.

Tennis Spectator Surprise

Sit side by side and synchronise head movements as though watching a tennis rally. One person breaks the sequence for a 'surprise' kiss – who is going to do it, and when?

Tête-bêche

This is a marvellous kiss – we *strongly* recommend you try it out. One person is lying on the sofa, the other person leans over them – the two heads are upside down with respect to each other. Concentrate on your partner's lips: the mouth will seem strangely reversed – which of course it is – and the chin will appear like a snout. Using a lip-liner or eyeliner pencil, mark on eyes, eyebrows, nostrils –

and possibly a moustache – around the snout. Keep talking during the approach to a kiss. This is extremely funny – your partner takes on a whole new personality.

That's Another Fine Mesh

Just try stretching a fishnet stocking (or a string bag sometimes used for oranges and the like) over your face when you kiss your partner ...

Theda Bara

It was said that this silent screen actress would glue herself onto a man and then drain the strength out of him. So enter the room where your partner is sitting comfortably, do not say a word, but approach with all the melodramatic gestures of this era (eyes open wide, head held back and look over left and right shoulders alternately with great flair.) Then show him a card on which are written the words KISS ME, MY FOOL! (from the film *A Fool There Was* (1915)). Proceed to zap the living daylights out of him.

Theoretical Kiss #1 – The Conceptual Kiss

'Theoretical Kisses' are kisses which, for one reason or another, cannot actually be performed. They are therefore kisses which one might put into writing at the end of a love-letter, or they may be dropped into a conversation. Here are some examples: The Conceptual Kiss involves choosing a concept from philosophy, mathematics, science, literary criticism or any other field of knowledge, and then describing a kiss carried out in the manner of the concept. For example, 'The Gödelian Kiss':

a kiss that takes an extraordinarily long time, yet leaves you unable to decide whether you've been kissed or not. Or 'The Heisenbergian Kiss': the more it moves you, the less sure you are of where the kiss was; the more energy it has, the more trouble you have figuring out how long it lasted.

Theoretical Kiss #2 – The Impracticable Kiss

Kisses of this type *might* be performed, but are beyond the abilities or means of most people. For example, 'The Rodeo Kiss': both ride bucking broncos and attempt to bring your lips together. Or 'The Tumbling Kiss': both do gymnastic tumbles across a mat towards each other and on your last tumble your lips meet in exactly the right position for a kiss.

Theoretical Kiss #3 – The Immortal Kiss

In this, you have to find a way of describing a kiss that goes on forever. For example: 'We will keep on kissing until the discovery of the last digit of pi.'

There's a 'K' in the Month, So ...

Say to the kissee, whom you have possibly just met, 'I have only one rule – I never kiss when there's a "K" in the month.' Immediately plant a smacker – and let it dawn on them that there are no months with 'K' in.

Thinker, The

If you catch your partner resting their head on their hand, then hold their head, take away the hand, kiss the place where the hand was, then replace the hand in its 'thinking position'.

Thumbelina, Stumbleina

In parts of California, and also in Helena, Montana, there is a superstition that you should kiss a person's thumb when they stub their toe. (Whether they will *appreciate* your reviving a piece of folklore at a time when they are in agony is another question, however ...)

Thumbnail Kiss

This is a common method of swearing an oath in Catholic countries – and you might want to use it with your partner when you want them to believe something unbelievable. The thumbnail is kissed and at the moment when this is done, the forefinger rests against the thumb; but immediately afterwards, the hand is moved away from the lips and the forefinger is simultaneously shifted down to the middle of the thumb. As a result, the thumb and forefinger now form a cross. This gesture is sometimes accompanied by the Spanish words, 'Por esta, la cruz – Te lo juro.' (By this, the cross, I swear it.)

Tia Maria Kiss

- $\frac{1}{2}$ oz Tia Maria
- $\frac{1}{2}$ oz amaretto
- crushed ice
- cream

Fill bottom half of a liqueur glass with crushed ice.

Mix together Tia Maria and amaretto and pour over ice.

Float a layer of cream over top.

Tic-Tac Tumble

This is cool ... or, at least, a parody of cool. The idea is that you make the kissee wait a few moments before kissing them – and during those moments, you open your mouth and let them see a small candy such as a Tic-Tac 'tumble' on your tongue. Only then do you close your mouth and kiss. (To get a deliberate clash of moods, you might suddenly kiss with unduly impatient passion.)

Tight-lipped

Person A places their lips inside Person B's lips. Then Person B exerts pressure inwards on A's lips, while Person A tries to exert as much pressure outwards on B's lips. Both should try to exert as much pressure as possible.

Timeless

You assume kissing position and then you both freeze. No movement at all – not even a blink! (If, as we did, you try this out in a public place, you'll probably attract some comments from onlookers, wondering what the hell you're up to!)

Tiny Brush Kiss

This kiss will completely change your experience of kissing a stubbly man. First of all, the female partner opens her mouth and places her lips lightly on either side of her partner's mouth to get the feel of the stubble. If he then splutters his lips (as in **Stalled Outboard Motor**) and she places her open mouth on his mouth again, the feel of the stubble is entirely different – like a tiny brushing on her lips.

Tongue Tickle Torture

Kissee extends tongue. Kisser moves tip of his tongue quickly from side to side on kissee's tongue – this is very ticklish for the kissee. Keep going for as long as the kissee can stand it.

Tongue Twister

Repeat the phrase 'Kisser kisses kissee' quickly over and over again, and when you collapse into gibberish, do some real tongue-twisting by putting your mouths together.

Tongue Wrestling

Stick out your tongue from the middle of your mouth. Your partner does the same. Put tongues together and exert pressure in opposite directions – the aim is to push your 'opponent's' tongue to one corner, as in arm-wrestling.

Tongue-lashing

Not everyone can do this: Curl up your tongue so that the tip is behind the top row of your teeth. Apply pressure until the tongue flicks out like a whip. Lash your partner's lips. (You could also try flicking the tongue out from your *lower* set of teeth. This isn't as powerful, but it is more manoeuvrable – you can flick from the side of your mouth, for instance.)

Touch of Class

Approach kissee with a rather condescending look and announce, 'I'm going to *basiate* you.' ('Basiate' being an *extremely* rare word for a kiss.)

Touch of Glass

Before handing someone a drink, kiss the rim of the glass – you might even put a lipstick mark on it – then turn the glass round so the kissed part faces the person as you offer it, and say, 'I want you to drink from *that* side.'

Touch, But Don't Look

Blindfold your partner (or get them to shut their eyes.) Also, get them to cover their ears, so they can't hear you removing clothes or moving around. They must be seated and puckered. Then apply a part of your body – *any* part – very briefly to their lips. Can they correctly identity which part of you they have kissed?

Touching Kiss

A kiss found in the *Kama Sutra*: 'When a girl touches her lover's lips with her tongue, and having shut her eyes, places her hands on those of her lover, it is called the "touching kiss".'

Tough Love

Pretend to be extremely aggressive when you kiss your partner – you'll discover that this makes your kisses far more passionate. As a general rule, you can say: for ardour, go harder. (Another technique for getting the right 'mindset' for passion is to kiss your partner in such a way that any bystander would be *embarrassed* to be standing nearby.)

Travel Kiss

(This 'scripted' kiss is rather like the famous Abbott and Costello sketch, 'Who's on First?') You ask your partner where in the world they would like to go to be kissed. The answer is 'Kissimee'. So you give a kiss and repeat the question. The same answer is given, so you kiss once more and again repeat the question, to which the answer is yet again, 'Kissimee', and so you kiss again ... Keep on with this routine, getting angrier and more insistent until eventually you yell: 'JUST TELL ME WHERE!' Kissee then answers, 'Kissimee in Florida ...'

Tree-Climbing Embrace

From the medieval Indian love treatise, the *Koka Shastra*: 'If with sighs she stands with one foot on her lover's foot, puts the other on his hip, one arm round his waist and the other round his shoulder, so that when he kisses her she climbs as if climbing into a tree ... (this is called) the tree-climbing embrace.'

Tulsa, Oklahoma

This kiss should be done right now if you're reading this book with your partner: in Tulsa, the law requires you to breathe between kisses. So do this in an exaggerated way, so you stand no chance of being arrested. (By the way, no one – not even married couples – is allowed to kiss for more than three minutes in Tulsa. In Iowa, the law is more liberal – there, you can kiss for up to five minutes!)

Tunnel of Love

This was one of the earliest components of our kiss-sequences – calling out its title makes the kiss effective: one person protrudes lips to make a circular 'tunnel', the other inserts tongue once. Reverse roles.

Turn Someone's Head

Feel like fooling around? (And we mean *around.*) Start mouth-to-mouth. Person A stays still, Person B rolls his head round Person A's head – Person B keeps rolling until his lips are again in contact with Person A's lips. (Even if this takes more than one circuit of Person A's head.)

Two Coins, The

The code is established that, when two coins are rubbed together with 'heads' in contact , it means a kiss. Do this across a room, moving the coins between thumb and fore-finger, so that your partner sees.

Uncomfortable, The

Kiss, and shift your body during that kiss, so that your partner is placed in an extremely uncomfortable position – as uncomfortable as possible. (If your partner really loves you, he'll maintain the kiss.)

Unicellular Union

A good conversational ploy to get onto the subject of kissing is to mention that animals, as well as humans, kiss: a male mouse licks the female's mouth, chimps even French-kiss, inserting their tongues, while elephants brush their trunks against their partners' lips. But to take this to the extreme, you could remark, 'Even *amoebas* do it … so why don't we?' You could explain that tiny one-celled organisms are known to link their mouths temporarily in order to exchange their hereditary nuclei; indeed, this may be the ultimate origin of kissing.

Vacuum Cleaner

This can be pretty painful – but worth doing occasionally for its shock-value. Kisser sucks *very* hard on lips of kissee, taking both lips inside mouth. Kisser then pulls back, still sucking.

Vampire to Vampire

Both extend your tongues and kiss sensuously, just touching tongue-tips. (The idea is to avoid the fangs.)

Vibro Kiss

Kisser puts hand behind head of kissee and vibrates the head back and forth against his mouth.

Voyeur, The

You both go to a place where you are likely to see some kissing couples. (The beach, public transport, amusement parks, etc.) When you spot a kissing couple, stare at them, trying to get as close as possible … and kiss to avoid getting caught!

Vulcan

Do the Vulcan salute palm to palm. (That is, both hold up a hand with a gap between second and third finger.) Your lips meet in the gap. Or: both hold up a hand, palm towards your own face, fingers spread in the Vulcan salute. Kiss the palm once and then turn the palm to face your partner. Bring the palms together. One person comments, 'Illogical ...'

Waiter

Kiss your palm and 'present' this kiss to your partner with a slight bow, as if you are presenting a platter. Your partner then kisses the palm.

Walking the Plank

This is the same type of kiss as **Slam Dunk** and **Ski Jump** – you might indeed want to link the trio together as a sequence: Person A protrudes tongue as 'plank'. Person B 'walks' his tongue in steps along A's tongue, getting closer to the tip. B's tongue then falls off and slides down A's chin.

Walrus

Both hold two fingers in front of the mouth in an inverted 'V'. Kiss in between the fingers. (If there's a sports team out there called the Walruses then how about adopting this as your official victory kiss?

War of the Worlds – Peace at Last

In H.G. Wells' novel *The War of the Worlds*, the Martian invaders are described as having a peculiar V-shaped mouth with a pointed upper lip. It takes practice, but if you suck in the left and right of your upper lip, while allowing the central part of the lip to remain forward, you can indeed form such a V-shaped lip. When you have mastered the technique, seek out an Earthling for an interplanetary kiss!

Water Ox

No, not a buffalo. You are both in a swimming pool. One person lies on their back, arms and legs outstretched to make an 'X', while the other swims around him/her in an 'O'. (That is, a 'hug'.)

Weights and Measures

The imperial system of kiss measurement is defined as follows:

   1 peck = a kiss lasting $\frac{1}{2}$ second
   1 smack = a kiss lasting 4 pecks
   1 snog = a kiss lasting 6 smacks.

Approach your partner pedagogically and demonstrate the system.

Wet T-shirt

Place a moistened tissue or kitchen towel against your lips. Kiss. (The strangest aspect of this kiss is that you taste water, rather than saliva, as your lips come together – it's quite a shock.)

While You Were Sleeping ...

If you find your partner asleep, kiss them *very* gently, so that they do not wake up. When they awake, boast of how many kisses you stole! Or, if you find your partner asleep, sneak up and give them a kiss – only, a *really* hard one so that they wake up. Then say, 'Why did you wake up on that one? That's twenty-seven.' Be all innocent. Will they believe you, or won't they?

Who's a Good Boy, Then?

Hold up your hand in the silhouette of a dog's head. (That is, first three fingers together, thumb up for 'ear' and pinkie moving up and down for mouth.) Say to your partner in a baby-voice, 'Nice little puppy wants to come and give you a lick.' Move the hand closer, and as you approach, stick your tongue through the puppy's mouth and lick your partner's face. (Of course, your partner may give your hand a slap and say, 'Bad dog!') This might seem one of the silliest kisses of all; nonetheless, for us this kiss has never really gone away – and 'little puppy' often puts in an appearance, for instance as the explanation of something going wrong. ('Little puppy dropped that wine-glass on the floor and broke it!') We also recommend this kiss in the swimming-pool: do doggie-paddle towards your partner – he/she says, 'Nice little puppy wants to come and give me a kiss ...'And when you reach him/her, do the puppy-lick hand.

Widow's Kiss

- 1 oz brandy
- $\frac{1}{2}$ oz yellow Chartreuse
- $\frac{1}{2}$ oz Benedictine
- dash bitters

Shake all ingredients with ice, strain into a cocktail glass and serve.

Wiper, The

This can be very sexy indeed. Your partner is wearing lipstick and you approach her with a tissue in your hand. Stare into her eyes and, rather forcefully, wipe the lipstick off. Then kiss the lipstick-marks on the tissue.

Witchdoctor

Both partners balance a pen between upper lip and nose to represent a bone through the nose. (This may take several attempts – you have to stick out your upper lip and press upwards to hold the pen in place.) Approach each other and kiss – but you mustn't let the bone fall!

With Gay Abandon

A dramatic pose for a kiss. Stand face to face. The first person throws their arms wide open and holds them out stiffly behind the back. That person also throws back their head. The other person grabs the wrists of the thrown-back arms and kisses the topmost point they can reach – about cleavage-level.

Within You, Without You

Think you've done everything possible with your mouth? Then try this: Person A puckers, then Person B's mouth encloses Person A's mouth. Person B's lips squeeze together, then Person A's mouth slips out of Person B's 'grasp'. Person A then encloses Person B's mouth and the process repeats, alternating the roles of 'grasper' and 'graspee.'

Wizard of Oz

Click your heels together three times and say, 'There's no place like ... .' and kiss your partner.

World Record Kiss #1

The world record for sustained kissing is 17 days $10\frac{1}{2}$ hours, set by Eddie Levin and Delphine Chra in Chicago, on 24 September 1984. If you don't feel like enduring this marathon just to break the record, then kiss in front of a day-a-page calendar, and sustain the kiss while you rip off 18 days.

World Record Kiss #2

The world record for total kisses in a two-hour period is 20,010, set by Jim Patterson and Toni Smith, on 17 August 1976 on Brighton Pier, England. (They were kissing lip to cheek, and one person pecking at a time.) If you don't want to go for the full two hours, then try the two-minute challenge, whereby you kiss at the world-record rate of one kiss every 0.35 seconds.

World Record Kiss #3

The world record for kissing underwater is 2 minutes 32 seconds, set on 18 February 1989 at the Ramada Hotel, Brighton, England by Tony Charman and Kim Vermley. If you don't want to go to the pool for your own attempt – or if you can't swim – then simply hold a glass of water above your heads while kissing, so that you are literally kissing *under water*.

X Marks the Spot

Simple, but effective, especially as a 'farewell' kiss: make an 'X' on the kissee's cheek with your fingertips.

X-it

Sitting in, say, a bar with your partner? Then try out this piece of kiss-choreography. Both raise an index finger and cross them to make an 'X'. (The fingers should be 'hooked' around each other, so that when you pull your hand towards you, you pull your partner's hand as well.) Take turns to pull your partner's side of the X to your lips to kiss: with each kiss, the two of you also come closer together, until your mouths are on either side of the X. Then pull your fingers away so your mouths meet.

X-Man, The

Which kiss can be seen from farthest away? Probably this one: stand and spread out your arms and legs so that your whole body forms one big 'X'.

X-Rated

Use your imagination for this one ... and remember there are some activities, and directions you may go, which require you to be over the age of consent! (If you want some ideas to stimulate the imagination, you might examine *The Encyclopedia of Unusual Sex Practices* by Brenda Love, Barricade Books, New York, 1992.)

X-Ray Eyes

Gently kiss your partner's eye – eyelid closed, of course! – and get them to move their eyeball in the pattern of an 'X' while you're doing it.

Y

Yakut

When these people of North-East Asia kiss, the nose is pressed on the cheek, a nasal inspiration follows during which the eyelids are lowered and lastly there is a smacking of the lips. These three phases are clearly distinguished.

Yammer Kiss

One person keeps on saying, 'Give me a kiss,' in an extraordinarily whining, peevish, complaining way – saying it fast, over and over again, like a spoilt brat. The only way to shut them up is to do what they want, and give them that kiss.

Yes!!!

This is an Algerian alternative to raising a fist in triumph: if you've solved a problem, kiss your own palm and then hold the hand with fingers vertical in front of your face. (A variation used in some Arab societies involves kissing the knuckle of the hand, then rotating the hand so that the palm is facing upwards. At the same time the eyes are raised to heaven – this is offering a kiss of thanks to the deity.)

You Kissed Yours

Look at each other's faces and interlock the fingers of your hands. (One hand each.) Squeeze hands, then one of you brings the hands towards the face for a quick kiss on the other's finger ... sounds easy, but you will find that if you look at the knuckles of the interlocked hands, it is actually quite difficult to instantly distinguish your partner's hand from your own. You may end up kissing your *own* finger by mistake.

You Turn My Dial

The whole point of this kiss is that it will probably fail ... but if it comes off, wow! Turn the dial of the radio, and go through the wavebands. You are trying to find a song – playing at that very moment – with a lyric that mentions kissing. If you do hear such a lyric, kiss your partner ... and tell him/her about the really strong feeling that you had that there would be such a song playing. If you fail ... well, try again another time.

Yum, Yum

As you kiss your partner, say 'Yum Yum' *very* quietly – so quietly that at first they can't hear what you are saying. When they realise, it will be all the sexier.

Zenoian

A kiss for philosophers: your lips approach your partner's lips, getting closer and closer, but never actually touch.

Zipper

An appropriate kiss to close the book: Person A has mouth tightly shut. Person B inserts his tongue in corner of A's mouth and moves along: A's mouth opens as B's tongue reaches the other corner. Then the tongue moves back and the mouth shuts.

BIBLIOGRAPHY

A History of Courting – E.S. Turner, Michael Joseph, London, 1964.

Art of Folly, The – Paul Tabori, Prentice Hall International, London, 1961.

Art of Kissing, The – William Cane, St Martins Press, New York, 1995.

Do's & Taboo's Around the World – Edited by Roger E. Axtell, John Wiley & Sons, New York, 1993.

Encyclopedia of Religion & Ethics – Edited by James Hastings, 1914

Etiquette – Emily Post, Cassell, London, 1969.

How Did Sex Begin – R Brasch, Angus & Robertson, Sydney, 1973.

Irish Wake Amusements – Sean O'Suilleabhain, Mercier Press, Cork, 1967.

Koka Shastra – Translated by Alex Comfort, George Allen & Unwin, London, 1964.

Mammoth Book of Oddities,The, Robinson Books, 1996.

North Carolina Folklore – Edited by Paul G. Brewster *et al*, Cambridge University Press, London, 1952.

On Kissing – Adrianne Blue, Victor Gollancz, 1996.

Recipes Web Site-http://soar.Berkeley.EDU/recipes

A Calendar of German Customs – Richard Thonger, Oswald Wolff, London, 1966.

Sexual Life of Savages, The – Bronislaw Malinowski, Routledge & Kegan Paul, London , 1932.

Snogging – Simon Mayo, HarperCollins, 1992.

Study of Games, The – Elliot M. Avedon & Brian Sutton-Smith, John Wiley & Sons, New York, 1971.

Victorian Parlour Games for Today – Patrick Beaver, Peter Davies, 1974.

World's Strangest Customs, The – E Royston Pike, Odhams Books, London, 1966.